BAD SCHOOL

By

Brenda P Boulter

Published in 2009 by YouWriteOn.com

Published by YouWrightOn.com

For my Family and Friends

Acknowledgements

Special thanks to Erin and Natasha for their help in the early stages.

Grateful thanks to Brenda for her invaluable proof reading.

Thanks also to Brenda and Anne from Vixon Fiction for their continuing help and support.

Chapter 1 – BULLIES

When I was a little girl, I always thought that ghosts wore old-fashioned costumes, like in history books; that they would look scary and walk through walls, leaving a chill in the air. But our ghost, if she really was a ghost, looked as real as you or me and she was as kind and helpful as a fairy godmother. Perhaps we invented her because we needed someone – we'll never know. But one thing we do know is that we'll never forget her. Perhaps I'd better start at the beginning.

*

Seneta, my best friend, was fidgeting.

'Keep still,' I hissed. 'It won't be long now.'

'But, Lotttie, my bum's gone numb,' she grumbled. 'Anyway, how do you know they'll come in here?'

'Shhh, I just do.'

Although it wasn't my idea of spending Wednesday lunchtime either – squashed in a girls' loo, listening to the drip – drip - drip of a tap that hadn't been turned off properly. I was thinking of my ham sandwiches, neatly packed in their plastic container, waiting in my locker just begging to be eaten. It was all right for Seneta, she had somewhere to sit but I was pressed up against the door, with a toilet roll holder digging into my back.

Some girls came in, laughing and chattering, noisily. I think they were making each other's faces up because there was a lot of giggling and shrieking.

1

'Keep still or I'll poke your eye out,' one girl said.

'Can I try your new lipstick?' asked another, who sounded like a Fourth Former. Even though their teacher was bound to make them wash it off, they were having more fun than us.

All went quiet when they left; apart from the annoying tap. *Drip, drip, drip.*

I began to think Seneta was right when our hideaway suddenly echoed with voices we recognised.

'Did you see Carrie's face when I threatened to stamp on it?' That was big mouth Tara Walker.

'And how purple it went, when I twisted her ear?' said the other one, Katy Underwood, cackling like an old witch.

'How much dosh did she cough up?' Tara asked, loud enough for the whole world to hear.

We heard the jingle of coins.

'Ten, twenty, thirty, fifty and three pennies - only fifty three pence this time,' said Katy, her tinny voice bouncing off the tiled walls.

'That's not much; we'll have to put the screws on harder tomorrow.'

'Yep. We'll teach her a lesson she'll never forget. That will serve her right for making friends with that Lottie Long-knickers and her sidekick.'

That did it. We burst out of the loo and, as planned, I grabbed Tara and Seneta got Katy. We dragged them into separate loos, kicking and screaming.

'Not so brave now are we? I said, holding Tara over the toilet. 'This is what you get for bullying 'First Years'.'

A sickly grin spread over Tara's face so I pressed her head down and pulled the chain, flushing water over her long golden locks. She wasn't smiling when I dragged her to the mirror.

'Oh dear, what a mess we've made,' said Seneta, in mock horror, hanging on to Katy, who was also dripping, and snivelling too. She had bits of pink toilet paper on the front of her white shirt.

Tara uttered words more suitable to a farmyard. She gave me a kick on the shin, which really hurt.

'Language girl, language!' I replied, gritting my teeth through the pain. 'You really must learn some manners.'

'Now how about returning that money?' said Seneta. Katy answered by biting her arm.

Seneta squealed and let Katy go but I grabbed her and held them both by the hair. They wriggled and squirmed in a most unladylike manner, while watching the door hoping someone would come in. Tara called my friend something I didn't hear, which made her furious.

She pulled some scissors out of her pocket and arched her black eyebrows in a devilish manner. She was holding the scissors open, like a crocodile ready to snap its jaws tight shut on its victim. Tara had lovely, naturally curly hair, I have to admit, and she knew it. She was always brushing it and admiring herself in the mirror. It made mine look as if it had been cut with a lawnmower.

'Why not?' I asked innocently, giving it an extra yank. 'It needs a trim.'

'You wouldn't dare.'

'Do it Seneta,' I urged.

With one tight squeeze and a metallic snap, Seneta cut a chunk out of those golden locks and held it up, like a prize.

'You dirty rotten rats!' Tara shouted, along with a few more words I couldn't possibly repeat.

Seneta's face was a mixture of horror at what she'd done and pride because she'd always been afraid of Tara.

'Your turn Katy,' she said, scissors poised for the second cut. There was no stopping her now.

'PUT THAT GIRL DOWN!'

Mr Murphy's eyes were nearly popping out of his head behind his bottle top glasses. He was mopping beads of sweat from his forehead and the lump in his long neck was bobbing up and down. (My mum says it's called an Adam's apple but his looked more like a conker, which he might swallow any minute). We let go of the girls as hair and scissors fell to the floor.

'WHAT DO YOU TWO THINK YOU ARE DOING?' he yelled, pulling his tie loose and unbuttoning the top button of his purple shirt. His face was so flushed, it was difficult to tell where the shirt ended and his neck began. I looked down at the floor. Tara's hair lay like a golden question mark by my foot.

'Just messing about Sir.'

Seneta twirled a piece of her own long black hair round her finger and put it between her teeth muttering:

'Yes, that's right Sir, only messing about,'

'Are you all right Tara? What happened?' he asked, between gasps of breath.

'They've been bullying us for ages,' said Tara, snivelling.

'That's not true,' I said, suddenly finding a high-pitched voice I didn't know I owned. She's such a liar!

'**BE QUIET!**' shouted Mr Murphy, making me jump.

'We're frightened to go out on our own,' added Katy as, wide eyed and pouting, she put her arm round her friend. I couldn't help thinking she would never get a part in the school play if she overacts like that at auditions.

'Or (sob) tell anyone,' added Tara from under her new, not very straight fringe.

The door swung open and Carrie West walked in. Whew, what a relief. She was the girl who had been bullied. She had asked for our help and was bound to clear us.

'Oh Carrie,' I said. 'Tell Mr Murphy what these two have been doing to you.'

Carrie looked at me as if I was speaking Russian.

'Go on Carrie,' said Seneta. 'Tell him what you told us about them stealing from you and threatening you.'

'Why would they do that?' said Carrie, looking a picture of innocence. 'Tara is my cousin.'

I looked at Seneta. She looked at me. The penny dropped. It was a trick. We had been stitched up.

Mr Murphy told us, or rather bellowed at us, to go to our lessons. He couldn't wait to get out of there and I couldn't either.

'Guess what?' said Seneta breathlessly, when we flopped into our chairs back in the classroom.

'What?'

'I need a wee.'

The next day we waited outside the headmistress's office. I was hungry and couldn't wait for my tea. We always had lasagne on Thursdays. My mum makes the best lasagne in the world.

'It's so unfair,' said Seneta, biting her nails and inspecting her handiwork. 'We thought we were helping Carrie.'

'Yes but it was brill wasn't it?' I reminded her as I chewed hard on my gum and tried to ignore my tummy rumbling.

'I know,' she said, her big brown eyes lighting up as she remembered our victorious moment. 'They deserved it.'

'Too right!'

Once inside the office, I saw Katy first. Her face went red but her eyes burned with hate. Tara stood next to her and lifted her turned up nose a bit higher when she saw me. The grown-ups were sitting down – Tara's mum, Mr and Mrs Sharma (Seneta's parents) and ... oh no, my mum and dad! It's not the first time my mum has been called to school but she doesn't usually stay cross for long; I can always get round her. But my dad! That meant trouble with a capital T. He wouldn't be best pleased about being dragged out of work. He shouts really loud and he's always saying that me, and Josh my brother, are the cause of his bald patch. He glared at me with that wait-till-I-get-you-home-young-lady glare, looking *so* un-cool with his shirt tucked into his trousers.

Mr Murphy (conker under control) sat next to Miss Armitage, who looked at me over her half moon glasses. They were perched on the end of her nose and had chains hanging down the sides and round her neck, so that she couldn't lose them.

'Is it right you pushed Tara's head down the toilet, Charlotte?'

I held my hands behind my back and crossed all ten fingers. My eyes wandered round the neat office and my nose tingled at the smell of Pledge, or was it Mr Sheen? The edges of my mouth twitched because I wanted to laugh.

'No Miss Armitage.'

Well I wasn't going to own up to that was I? Anyway I couldn't say anymore, even if I'd wanted to. My chewing gum was stuck round the back of my teeth. A good time to look at my shoes, I thought.

'And did you push wet toilet paper into Katy's mouth Seneta?'

7

I nearly choked when I heard that. Good old Seneta. She also studied her shoes and I'll bet her fingers were crossed too.

'No Miss Armitage.'

'And you did nothing to provoke this incident Tara?'

As if.

'No Miss Armitage,' Tara replied smugly, all fingers uncrossed (and nails, clearly painted with *my* Sci-fi Silver nail polish that had gone missing two days earlier). She looked so innocent, like I Can't Believe it's not Butter wouldn't melt in her pretty (I don't think so) mouth. Oh pl-*ease*, I thought. She's got a bra on! My mum wouldn't get me a bra. She said I wasn't old enough, or big enough. She said I had to be 13 years old or 32-inch bust before she would even consider it. And here was Tara, sticking her 30A chest out (I can't honestly call it a *bust*) – a liar, thief and bully and she gets *rewarded*. Life sucks!

She gave me a sideways glance, twisting it into that slimy grin which makes her look like a cartoon cat, and tossed her bouncy curls like an advert for shampoo. She'd been to the hairdressers and they had made a good job of covering up Seneta's handiwork. Trust her to go down the toilet and come up smelling of KC One.

Tara's mum, all dolled up like a dog's dinner, put her twopenn'orth in.

'*And* they cut her hair. Hooligans, that's what they are. They don't belong in a school like this. It cost me an arm and a leg at the hairdressers' last night. It's the parents I blame.

8

Some people ought to have more control over their children. More discipline, that's what I say.' Her voice rose higher with every sentence and she looked at my mum as if she was dog poo.

Mum was sniffing into her hankie. I love her to bits but when she cries, her mascara runs and she looks like a panda. Dad had two red apples for cheeks, but he didn't say anything. (Bad sign, *really* bad sign). Seneta's parents sat stiff and proud. Their dark faces didn't give away what they were thinking. I suspected that would come later, when they got home.

Tara dropped her hankie on the floor and made a big show of picking it up, causing her black trousers to stretch over her bottom. I soon understood why. Oh *rea*-lly – she was wearing a *thong* – with *diamantes!* I don't believe it.

'Are you listening to me Charlotte?' said Miss Armitage in a shrill voice, making me jump. Her eyes bore into me as if she could see right through me.

'Yes Miss Armitage.'

I wasn't *really* listening. She was going on and on, like grown ups do, about letting down my parents, letting down the school, blah, blah... My mind started to wander in the direction of my stomach again. We wouldn't get any tea at this rate. I might even die of hunger, right in front of them – that would serve them right. I wondered what was for pudding and hoped it was lemon meringue pie.

Suddenly I saw a look of horror on Seneta's face. My mum went pale, and Dad's head fell forward. Katy's eyes bulged as she looked at Tara. Tara's grin got wider, like a cat that got the extra thick double cream. Seneta's mum and dad looked at one another in disbelief and Mr Murphy's conker was bobbing up and down in his neck. I felt as if I was watching a movie in slow motion. From somewhere far away, I heard Miss Armitage's voice:

'So you see, we've decided to make an example of you. We're sending you away to Grimstone Priory. It's a school, in the South of England, for girls with behaviour problems. What have you got to say for yourselves?'

Behaviour problems? I certainly had something to say about *that*. But for once nothing would come out. There was a lump in my throat as big as Mr Murphy's conker and it wasn't only the chewing gum that I'd just swallowed. My eyes were stinging and the room went blurry. I stuck out my chin and tightened my lips, to stop the bottom one quivering like strawberry jelly.

No way! They couldn't do this! Tara and Katy were the bullies. They were evil. At Junior School, Tara and Katy used to wait outside and pull my ponytail, kick me and call me Ginger Longbottom stupid daughter of Mr Shortbottom (My proper name is Longfellow, like the poet). And they would take our homework and copy it. Once, when Seneta was only eight, they beat her up, just because she's Indian and different from them. They threatened to put fireworks through her letterbox if she told anyone the truth. We'd waited a long time to get our own back.

10

But when we started big school we grew taller than Katie and Tara. We soon learned how to stick up for ourselves and found out that bullies are cowards. Very soon other kids asked us for help and we were only too happy to oblige. The trouble is that cowards tell lies. And, because Katy and Tara were smaller than we were, teachers believed them, not us.

I looked at Seneta. Her big brown eyes looked so scared, like a frightened puppy. I felt just as scared as she did. And I didn't feel hungry any more.

BAD SCHOOL

Chapter 2 – WAITING

'JOSH, PACK IT IN!' I shouted. 'Mum – Tell him.'

'Josh, don't annoy your sister,' she said absently, while she was knitting me a new grey cardigan for my new grey school.

He took no notice. He'd bought one of those horrible snakes dangling from a stick on a length of elastic and kept teasing me with it while I was trying to play on the computer.

I had spent two weeks grounded since my suspension from school. Two whole weeks being unpaid help and general dogsbody! My fingernails were cracked from washing up (I hate Mum's Marigolds, they remind me of the dentist). My arms swung like a monkey's after all the shopping I'd carried. I had even cleaned Josh's bedroom twice but flatly refused to go in there again after I trod on something squishy in a plastic bag. I knew I shouldn't look inside but even so I nearly threw up when the putrid smell invaded my nostrils. Apparently my disgusting brother had been experimenting with worms and just 'forgot' they were there.

Now that the holidays had officially started, I was bored.

'*Please* can I go round to Seneta's house?' I begged for the zillionth time.

Mum sighed.

'Oh go on then. But be home before your dad gets in at 6 o'clock, or else he'll go bananas.'

I jumped for joy and wrapped my arms around her, knocking some stitches off her needle. On my way past Josh I grabbed the snake. He held onto the stick and the elastic stretched longer and longer. I was about to flirt it at him when I heard a crack. The stick had broken. I dropped the snake and ran like mad. As I slammed the door, I could hear his whiney voice.

'Mu-um – look what Lottie's done!'

Tell tale.

*

I pressed the bell on the shiny red door and waited for someone to answer. When the door opened, it wasn't Seneta or her parents who stood there but a very handsome, very tall hunk, with smouldering brown eyes.

'I, I've come to see Seneta,' I stammered like a ten year old. (I should have had more self control at twelve and three quarters).

'She's in the kitchen, helping her mother.' He had a beautiful deep velvet voice – I was in love. 'Go on in, I'm off now.' Reluctantly, I watched him go.

Seneta was pleased to see me but her mum looked a bit cross. She said that Seneta wasn't allowed out, and didn't look too pleased when I asked if I could stay. She clicked her tongue and said: 'Just for half an hour then.'

'I'm in love,' I announced, when we reached Seneta's bedroom. 'Who was he - that boy who let me in? He's drop dead gorgeous!'

'Oh, that's my cousin, Danesh. You can put your eyes back in their sockets. He's getting married soon.'

'No way! What's she like?'

'I don't know; he's not met her yet.'

I'd heard about arranged marriages. I wondered what Seneta felt about it.

'Will you have an arranged marriage?' I asked, curious now.

'I expect so,' she replied, shrugging her shoulders like she'd never thought about it.

It seemed weird to me. Like missing out on all the romantic stuff and going straight to the boring part.

'How awful.'

'I think all boys are gross anyway so I don't suppose it will matter.'

I didn't believe that for a minute.

'What about Toby Ferguson then?' I knew she fancied him.

'Well I won't see *him* again will I?' she said, miserably.

I had to agree that going to an all girls' school did lessen our chances on the romantic front. I started brushing Seneta's long hair in front of her bedroom mirror. It was jet black and shiny, unlike my dull red spiky cut.

'They're not going to keep you in for the whole six weeks are they?'

'Probably,' said Seneta, with a sigh, 'Apart from going to the Temple.'

'Can't you stand up to them a bit more?' I asked, looking round the room at the Barbie

15

wallpaper and matching quilt. 'Tell them you're growing up?' She almost seemed frightened of her parents. My dad is strict but I'm not frightened of him. Like he doesn't give big hugs or anything but he calls me Princess and ruffles my hair. (I wish he wouldn't do that actually, but Mum says it's because he loves me). And Mum, well Mum is just cuddly Mum. I can tell her anything and she understands (most of the time). I love her to bits. Did I say that already?

'Oh I don't mind really,' she said. 'I would rather stop in than go to that horrible school. Why can't we go to another school in Derbyshire? I mean – Grimstone Priory. What sort of a name is that? It sounds awful, and so far away. And it's probably full of the most terrible girls in the country – you know - the dregs of society. It's not fair.'

I agreed with her. It was rotten luck to be sent to an all girls' school, just when boys were becoming interesting. Something must happen to change them from little horrors like Josh into boy band types like Danesh. I couldn't imagine someone as dishy as him picking his nose or having burping contests with his friends.

'It might not be that bad,' I said, hopefully. 'A priory is a sort of monastery and they are supposed to be lovely, peaceful places. They probably think it will quieten us down.

She nodded, thoughtfully.

'Perhaps there'll be a boys' school nearby,' I went on. 'And we could meet fantastic looking hunks after dark and have midnight feasts.'

She started to look interested, until I said:

'It may even have a ghost.'

Me and my big mouth! I'd forgotten how frightened she was of all things scary. She snatched the brush from me and attacked her hair with strong hard strokes as if it was somehow to blame.

'Let me do your nails,' I said, fishing a new bottle of Stunningly Purple out of my pocket. 'Mum bought me some new polish. I could do patterns.'

'My mum will only make me take it off,' she answered miserably.

I shrugged and decided to tell her about Josh and me having a tug of war.

'That's horrible,' she said. She stopped brushing in mid stroke and looked hard at me. 'Mum's right, you *are* turning into a bully.' So, her mum blamed me then. I sniffed and bit my lip.

'No I'm not – it's what brothers and sisters do. It was his own fault - he shouldn't be such a pest. Anyway, on the way home I'll buy him some sweets and he'll forgive me.'

'You *are* lucky. I wish *I* had a brother or sister,' she said, with an even bigger sigh. She started biting her nails, which were already down to the quick. My nail varnish would have been wasted. She *was* depressed. Whatever I talked about seemed to upset her. It didn't make sense. She was the lucky one – having her parents all to herself. I had mine to myself until I was about six. I was adopted and that was cool. They thought they couldn't have kids and chose me. They made me feel really special.

Then Josh came along – a miracle they called it. It was nice having a baby in the house – like a doll that was real and warm, and smelled nice. Everyone said he was the spitting image of Dad, which made me feel a bit left out because I don't look like anybody. And just lately, Josh'd been having really good reports from school and everyone said how clever he was. I wanted them to be proud of *me*. Now, thanks to Tara and Katy, I'd really blown it. I didn't say any of this to Seneta though. I kept it to myself.

Suddenly I had an idea.

'Let's get our own back on Tara and Katy!'

'How?'

'Let's send them postcards from wherever we go, telling them what a wonderful time we're having.'

Seneta was puzzled.

'Believe me, it will bug them. And if we don't put stamps on, they'll have to pay double.'

'But we never go anywhere.'

'We've got a caravan holiday booked in Devon and aren't you going to London?'

Seneta's eyes showed a bit more sparkle.

'Yes, to my cousin's wedding. And another cousin is coming from India with my aunt and uncle. He might take one back and post it for us.'

'Cool! I don't know if it will work from another country but we can try. We'll give a card to anyone we know who's going away. Our neighbours are going to Disneyland!'

'Tara will be green with envy if she thinks *we've* been; her parents only take her to boring museums.' Seneta was getting into the mood.

'I'll buy some cheap cards with rude cartoons on them,' I said, giggling. 'What shall we write on them?'

Seneta shrieked.

'Having a great time. Glad you're *NOT* here!'

'How about – This place is a *CUT* above?'

Seneta fell back onto the bed and dissolved into fits of giggles.

'Do you know anyone who is going to *LOOE?*' she asked.

'No but I know someone who is going to *BOG-ROLL*!'

(Yes I *know* that was stupid but I couldn't think of anything else!)

'I hope it doesn't rain - they'll get *WET!*'

'I know, I know – Have a good life, hope you're FLUSHED with success!'

With that we both sank onto the pink duvet in hysterics. The bed became a bouncy castle. We started throwing pillows and teddies up in the air. We were laughing at nothing really but it was lovely to see Seneta happy again. Tears of laughter were streaming down her face.

A BANG BANG BANG on the bedroom door turned us into statues. Barbie and Ken shuddered and My Little Pony fell off the dressing table. We were still untangling ourselves from the bedclothes when Seneta's mum appeared.

19

'GET OUT!' she said. 'GET OUT OF THIS HOUSE. NO WONDER SENETA HAS BEEN LED ASTRAY - TEAMING UP WITH THE LIKES OF YOU. YOU'RE A BAD APPLE.'

I ran out of the house and down the street crying. I had never been called an apple before, bad or otherwise.

Chapter 3 – GRIMSTONE

The car tyres scrunched on the pebbles as we made our way up the long winding drive. I wriggled because my new knitted jumper was itchy. I could have done a pole dance naked in my blazer and no one would have seen anything, it was that big. Dad was admiring the avenue of trees.

'Limes, I think,' he mused.

Mum looked up at the canopy of leaves.

'I love this time of year, the changing colours are beautiful.'

They were acting as if it were a drive in the country instead of taking their daughter to God-knows-where. I wanted to scream.

'SPLAT' – Something green landed on the windscreen and it wasn't a leaf. Dad was about to flick the wipers on when

'NO!' I shouted, as I realised that a frog was splattered in front of our eyes. Mum screamed, her face changing to a shade of green similar to the poor creature. Dad stopped the car and while he was uttering some unmentionable words, I got out and lifted up the unfortunate animal. I could tell by the bad smell it had been dead for a while. It reminded me of Josh. Not the smell (well maybe the smell) but 7-year-old boys like that sort of thing. Good job we'd left him with Gran I thought as I looked around. All was quiet except for a slight rustle in the bushes nearby.

'Get in the car Lottie,' said Dad sharply.

'And put that thing down!' mum screeched, giving a shudder.

I did as I was told but not before copping a flying squashed tomato, right on the back of my head.

'So that's how it's going to be,' I muttered sulkily as I climbed back in.

When Grimstone Priory came into view I had a feeling that Seneta had been right all along. It was grim all right – and not at all like a monastery! With its tall towers and thin, pencil-like windows it looked evil.

'Gothic, I think,' Dad commented, in his matter of fact way.

Horrible stone creatures with wide-open mouths snarled at us from every corner of the building.

'What are they?' I asked as we got out of the car.

'Gargoyles,' he said, following my gaze. His lips were squeezed together and there were creases between his dark eyebrows.

I looked at mum but she was sniffing into her hankie. She did a lot of that lately. I was used to it, along with raised voices behind closed doors. I had to face it; I was a disappointment to them.

*

A girl with frizzy black hair met us at the door. She wore a pink dress that looked too tight over her (rather large) bust. I couldn't help looking down at myself. I was still aware of the new 32A bra Mum had bought me and stuck my chest out a little harder in an attempt to fill it. Mum had relented when I explained that I would be already thirteen by the time she saw me again and, to seal the argument, told her that even Seneta had one. (Which wasn't quite true but she was going to tell her mum the same about me.)

'I'm Toyah,' said the girl, while chewing on some gum with her mouth wide open. 'I'm a prefect see. You have to do what I say. I'll tek you up to the headmistress. Her name is Mrs Potts.'

She had a strange accent, a bit like Cilla Black. I must have been staring at her because she said:

'Want some?'

I shook my head, just as she blew a bubble that burst all over her face. I saw Mum out of the corner of my eye, giving one of her disgusted looks.

'What's she like – Mrs Potts?' I asked, as we climbed some stairs.

'Oh she's all right; she's not bothered what you do,' answered Toyah, pulling down her skirt, which insisted on riding back up her enormous thighs. 'So long as you don't burn the school down - you're not here for arson are you?'

'No,' I said, looking behind to see if Mum and Dad had heard. I needn't have worried though. They were too busy arguing about something.

'That's all right then. Only, if the police come sniffing round, Mrs Potts and her weedy little husband usually disappear for a while.'

Toyah walked straight in to the office, without even knocking. We followed. I expected it to look something like Miss Armitage's office but I couldn't be more wrong. It was a right mess.

Cardboard boxes were stacked everywhere and on the windowsill lay a half eaten sandwich, curled up at the corners.

Mrs Potts appeared to be looking for something among the piles of files and papers littering her huge desk.

'Welcome to Grimstone Priory er...'

'Charlotte Longfellow.'

'Oh, er, yes – Charlotte.'

Her purple hair and emerald green eye shadow made her look like a clown. Bright red lipstick was applied with a paintbrush, it seemed, and ran into the cracks round her mouth.

She turned to my parents and said:

'Don't worry about your daughter. She will soon settle down. Now I have some forms for you to sign, if only I can find them.'

She eventually found the papers that she wanted and they did the business. I felt as if I was being sold at the cattle market.

'Say goodbye to your parents Charlotte,' she said, tapping her long red nails on the desk. 'I'm sure they have much better things to do than sit here - like get on with their lives without you!'

That really hurt and she said it so sweetly that Mum and Dad didn't seem to notice. But it was all too quick. I thought they may be able to stay with me a while, at least until Seneta arrived with her mum and dad. I clung to Dad tightly.

'Try to be good Princess,' he said, with a gravely voice. His moustache tickled when he kissed me. Instead of laughing, my eyes went watery and there was a lump in my throat. I wanted to say things like 'You'll be proud of me one day,' but it got stuck and nothing would come out. I turned to look at Mum. My mouth said sorry but again, nothing came out.

'Oh my darling,' she said, and hugged me so tight I thought I would burst. Over her shoulder I saw Toyah putting two fingers in her mouth, pretending to vomit.

*

Feeling scared and trying hard not to blubber I followed Toyah down long echoey corridors. Everywhere was so quiet; I wondered where all the other pupils could be. The only people I saw were on paintings hung on the wood panelled walls. My bags felt like they were full of bricks but Toyah didn't offer to help.

'Is that really your name – Charlotte?' she asked. 'I think Ginger suits you better.'

'I hate being called Ginger. Everybody calls me Lottie,' I answered glumly.

She wriggled in the too tight dress.

'Don't upset yourself about your folks. They've probably forgotten you already. The first time I went back home for a holiday, my parents had moved and not even told me. That's how much they cared.'

I would most likely have burst into tears right there and then if it hadn't been for the noise. Toyah had just started to climb some stairs, with me following closely behind. The sound of crashing china, not to mention shouting and screaming, was coming from a room opposite. A plate flew through the door and smashed onto an already wonky picture of Henry the Eighth. Baked beans slithered down his smiling face.

'That's the Dining Room,' said Toyah, hurrying out of the way.

'Don't they get into trouble?' I asked, while ducking as a spoon narrowly missed my head. 'Where are the teachers?'

Toyah looked down at me as if I was something she had trod in.

'No, Stupid,' she said. 'What can they do? If *you* think you're going to turn over a new leaf, forget it. Don't you know it's a bad girls' school? **YOU *HAVE* TO BE BAD!'**

*

Toyah opened the door to my dormitory. There were six flat beds, each with a bedside table and not much else. I wished I'd brought my squishy pillow with me.

'That's your bed in the corner, next to the Asian.

Dropping my bags, I ran to greet my friend Seneta! I was so relieved to see her and suddenly felt less scared.

'Seneta's my best friend and she's Indian! You may be a prefect but, well watch it, that's all.'

'Ok, ok, Ginger. Don't get your knickers in a twist. It's no big deal.

'And I don't like being called Ginger!' I shouted crossly.

'Oops Sorr - yy!' said Toyah, not sounding like she meant it at all.

*

Toyah pushed past two girls as they walked in. The smaller of the two was holding a hankie against her forehead.

'I'm sure it was Penelope Freestone who took Prince,' she said. The voice sounded posh but a brace on her teeth caused her to lisp.

'Don't worry, Nat, you'll find another one,' said the taller dark haired one, who had glasses and a Birmingham accent like one of my grannies.

They suddenly noticed us.

'Hi! I'm Georgina and this is Natalie,' said the tall one. 'Nat's hurt. She collects bugs and anything nasty by the way, so it would be advisable to leave anything you find in a cardboard box well alone. Girls are always goading her because of her brace and they call me 'Specky Square Eyes,' which drives me wild. The food is disgusting but the mice are friendly. Oh, and the Police and Fire Department are regular visitors. Welcome to Hell!'

She pulled a face as she looked down on Natalie's head. Blood was running into her long blonde hair, reminding me of spaghetti bolognaise.

'I can't stand the sight of blood.'

'Here, let me help,' offered Seneta. 'I'm Seneta and this is Lottie.'

I got some tissues out of my bag and passed them to Seneta who dabbed gently on the cut. It was right up her avenue, she had always wanted to be a nurse like her mum.

'What happened to you Natalie?' I wanted to know.

'An argument with a plate. What's that in your hair?'

'Tomato,' I said. 'I copped it on the drive. Can't wait to get my hands on the culprit.'

Georgina looked us up and down.

'You look too smart. You'd better take those blazers off. No one wears them here. You stand out like fairies at a Halloween party, which by the way is not allowed here. Come to think of it nobody would notice the odd weirdo round here. Besides, it's a sure fire way to get detention.'

'What is?' I asked. It didn't make sense.

'Wearing school uniform - then if you get caught in the village doing anything you shouldn't, they will deny you belong to this school.'

No discipline and no uniform – strange. I thought I might be in a dream and wake up soon.

Two more girls came in. They were identical twins. They had squeaky voices and mousy hair that was tied in bunches on the top of their head. It made them look like two little rabbits. One of them wore pink round glasses and the other had hers in her hand and a squint in her eye, which was slightly swollen and going black.

'Oh my life!' she said.

'You too?' said Natalie.

'Yes and my glasses are broken. I can't see a thing without them!

'Meet Topsy and Flopsy,' said Georgina, taking the glasses to see what she could do.

'Hi,' I said, wondering if they were their real names but deciding this was not the time to ask. 'What happened?'

'Penelope Freestone, that's what!' said Flopsy, in a squeaky voice (or it might have been Topsy. You'll have to excuse me if I get them mixed up – I still can't tell them apart).

'What's a chav?' asked the one with the broken specs.

Georgina was not amused.

'Never mind,' she said and turned to me.

'There are always fights at mealtimes. Nat thought it was Penelope who took her pet frog but it's best to keep clear of her - she's in Grievous. We don't have anything to do with them.'

'Oh, Prince is a frog?' I said. It was slightly disappointing.

'What do you mean, Grievous?' asked Seneta, frowning.

'Like grievous bodily harm,' said Georgie. 'We have four houses in this school - one in each tower. The bullies go in 'Grievous'. Girls who set fire to things - mostly schools - go into 'Arson'. There's nothing flammable in there by the way.

'Thieves go in Klepto – short for Kleptomania,' added Topsy, 'like that horrible prefect Toyah Tranter. Keep clear of her. Light fingers Tranter we call her.'

I knew kleptomania meant stealing. I felt in my bag. My purse had gone! She must have taken it while I was hugging Seneta!

'She got you then?' said Flopsy, seeing the look on my face. 'Oh my life - she wants locking up!'

'And mine too!' wailed Seneta.

'Well of all the..'

29

Two enemies already and we'd only just arrived!

'What are you here for?' I asked.

'We hated school because we're no good at lessons. Everyone kept saying we were dumb, so we went shopping instead,' said Flopsy sadly.

'I used to bunk off because my parents were splitting up and I was so worried I couldn't concentrate.' Georgina added with a shrug. 'They're divorced now.'

'And I couldn't hear what the teacher was saying, so I didn't bother.' Natalie said, inspecting the bloodstained tissue. I passed her a second one, hoping they would forget to ask us why we were there.

'Why did you bunk off school then?' asked Georgina. She had just assumed we were truants.

'We hated the teachers,' I said, looking at Seneta.

'Yeah,' Seneta caught on quick. 'They were gross.'

'Wait till you see this lot here!' Georgina warned as she handed back Topsy's glasses. 'But in the meantime, welcome to Truant! It's the best house to be in. If there's anything you need, just ask.'

'I need the loo!' Seneta announced, urgently.

*

Seneta was worrying like my mum as we looked for the loo.

'What if they find out?'

'We'll have to hope they love us by then,' I joked.

30

'It's not funny. Grievous sounds horrible. This is a positively awful place,' she said sulkily, and gave a shudder.

I had to agree.

'Never mind. We'll look out for each other.'

'Yes.' Seneta smiled bravely. 'We'll stick together, no matter what.'

We had reached a door marked 'TOILET'. Seneta gingerly opened the door.

'I wonder if it has a ghost?' she whispered.

'You've been reading too much Harry Potter!' I teased and gave her a push.

I used the loo and washed my hands, throwing the paper towel towards the bin. It missed and landed on the floor.

'PICK THAT UP!'

Turning round, I expected to see a teacher standing behind me. Instead, it was a girl whose fair hair was tied back with a yellow ribbon. She wore pink rubber gloves and had a face of the same colour. She had obviously been cleaning the toilets.

'Sos,' I said, picking up the paper towel and placing it in the bin. 'Why are *you* doing that? Is it the cleaner's day off?'

'You must be new!' she replied, pursing her lips. 'This is their idea of punishment. You'll find out. I went to bed early instead of watching a horror video last night and one of the prefects saw me. You're not allowed to do anything good here. It's pants!'

Three girls burst in. Their behaviour was disgusting to say the least. They banged the doors

31

and didn't pull the chain. They didn't even wash their hands Ugh! A large girl with studs in her nose, lips and eyebrows was clearly the ringleader. The other two copied everything she did. They also had piercings but not so many. They drew faces on the newly cleaned mirror with lippy.

'Don't do that!' said the girl with the rubber gloves, angrily.

'Oooh, and who's going to stop me? Not that worm Melanie Pearson who's just crawled out of a lavatory pan?'

She turned to Melanie, and raised her fist as if she was going to beat her up. Melanie's red face turned white and she backed against the wall. I couldn't stand back and watch this.

'Try me!' I said.

I stood with my arms folded and glared my worst glare.

'And who do you think you are?' she said, curling her lip into a sneer. This made her spotty face look more ugly than ever.

'Lottie Longfellow as it happens. I've just arrived and I don't like bullies.'

'Well, Grottie Lottie. If you think you're going to be top dog, you'll have another think coming. No one gets the better of Penelope Freestone. By the way, call me Penny and your *dead*. Come on girls, let's go. We'll let you off this time but watch out - WE'LL GET YOU WHEN YOU LEAST EXPECT IT!'

They went out, slamming the door behind them.

'Wow, thanks!' said Melanie, sliding down the wall until she was sitting on the floor. She looked like she was going to be sick.

'Nice specimens of humanity,' I said. 'What do the other two call themselves?'

'The one with the purple top was Tina Feathers and the one with the Afro was Deirdre Richardson. They're always together. I've never seen anyone stand up to them before. Thanks again!'

'Don't mention it,' I sighed. I looked in the mirror and tried to get tomato pips out of my hair. 'I've got a feeling it won't be the last time.'

BAD SCHOOL

Chapter 4 – SETTLING IN

The following morning I stood with Seneta in a sleepy line. We were waiting to collect our breakfast and, surprisingly, there was no pushing and shoving like you'd expect in a school without proper rules. Apart from the odd girl pushing in, no one seemed to be in a hurry to get to the front. We were soon to find out why.

'Eggs or beans?' A gargantuan woman demanded. She had a white overall on with different colour splashes down the front. Her face looked like a sour Granny Smith apple. I looked down at the choice of food in the large metal containers. The scrambled egg swimming in grease was a funny orange colour. The baked beans, obviously no brand known to man, looked pale and uninviting. Mind you, the porridge alternative looked remarkably like the wallpaper paste Dad uses. Oh well.

'Beans please,' I said, holding out my brown wooden tray. She dolloped a spoonful of grey beans onto a grey chipped plate. Another, equally disgusting woman, with a cigarette hanging out of her mouth, slapped a black square on top of the beans and a third added a glass of orange coloured water, none too carefully, spilling most of the contents.

'Georgina was right,' I whispered to Seneta as we sat down at a long table. The food *is* disgusting.'

'What's the black thing?' asked Seneta, prodding it with a fork.

Before I could tell her it was toast, a sharp finger prodded me in the back.

'YOU'RE SITTING IN MY CHAIR!' said a voice I recognised. It belonged to Penelope Freestone. I looked round.

'No one was sitting here. There's plenty of room.'

She folded her arms and glowered.

'MOVE!'

The room went deathly quiet. All eyes were on us. I wasn't sure what to do. If I got up meekly, we would be bullied forever and not only by Penelope. However - if we stayed?

Deirdre and Tina joined her, carrying their breakfast trays.

'Let's go,' whispered Seneta.

I stood up slowly.

'That's it, shift and take Fart Face with you,' Penelope snarled.

That did it. No one gets away with insulting my friends. I lifted up my plate of beans under toast. I was just about to smash it into her face when Georgina called from across the room.

'Lottie, Seneta – over here! We've been saving seats for you!'

Seneta hurried over. I lowered the plate but my eyes were still locked with Penelope's.

'You'll keep,' I muttered. She treated me to her sickly grin, reminding me of Tara.

'That's it, Grottie Lottie,' she said. 'Go over to the loser's table. Specky Square-eyes and Jaws will look after you.'

I moved away but it is *so* not easy to move your chair and juggle with a tray of food at the same time. I pushed the chair out, scraping it on the floor. It "accidentally" caught Penelope's foot. She yelped and jumped back, knocking Deirdre's tray flying. Scrambled egg splattered all over Tina who, in turn, spilt orange juice onto another girl sitting behind.

'Watch it!' shouted the girl, who jumped up and pushed Tina.

'Leave her alone!' said Deirdre, grabbing the girl's nose and twisting it.

Penelope forgot about me and waded in to join the fight.

'What's up with her?' asked Natalie when I joined the others.

'Oh, she wanted to know if I knew a good plastic surgeon. She needs her face rearranging.'

Georgina nearly choked on a mouthful of scrambled egg. I passed her a drink of orange and when she had stopped spluttering she wiped bits of egg off her glasses saying:

'It's going to be fun, having you around.'

I looked at my new friends. Natalie smiled and the sun, streaming through the long dirty windows, glinted on her brace. The twins were sitting so close you would think they were joined. They're not losers, I thought. They were all looking at me with a sort of admiration, as if I was going to save them from something – I don't know what. I set to work attacking the slimy beans and black toast and tried not to think of Mum's creamy porridge.

*

Our first lesson was Maths. We followed Georgie and the gang into Room 31 wondering what to expect. The noise was deafening. Natalie was in front of us and when she went in, the room fell silent. She turned and shouted 'RUN' to us but it was too late. Seneta and I caught the full force of a bucket of ice-cold water. The room was in uproar as we ran like mad down the corridor bumping straight into a teacher. She blinked slowly behind her huge round glasses like a wise old owl. It was Miss Orrell the maths teacher.

'I can see you're soon fitting into school life,' she said, patting the brown bun at the back of her head. 'Go and get changed and we'll see you later.'

I couldn't believe it. She didn't even bat an owl's eyelid.

'Did you see Penelope Freestone's face?' said Seneta when she was pealing her wet jeans off. 'I wonder how they did it. I mean to say, Georgie and the others walked through and nothing happened.'

'I saw a length of string when it was too late.' I was trying to undo my beloved bra that was sticking to me as if I had been born in it. 'She must have been waiting for us but she needn't think she's going to get away with it,'

'Oh blimey,' wailed Seneta. 'Where do they send girls who are naughty at a bad girls' school?'

She yammered on about Detention Centres for delinquents but I was already wondering how to get my own back.

*

Georgina was *so* right about the food – yuk! It was a punishment in itself – big time. We called the cook and her two assistants the three witches.

The first dinner we were fed out of the witches' cauldron consisted of overcooked cabbage, lumpy mashed potatoes and cheese pie, which smelled like my brother's trainers. I wondered whether to eat it or launch it and I now understood the reason for the food fights. I inwardly cried for Mum's steak and kidney pie with its juicy mushrooms, succulent velvet brown gravy and fluffy mashed potatoes like summer clouds.

After a few days, Seneta and I decided to write home.

Dear Josh,

Hi. I just thought I'd write and tell you what a crappy school this is. It is pants! The food is horrible and we have to watch horror videos every night. I expect you'd like that, but I think they're boring and they make Seneta have nightmares. You're not ALLOWED to be good here! No kidding! A cross-eyed dumpy teacher called Miss Goldsmith teaches us CRIMINOLOGY. That is about famous people committing crimes like Ronnie Biggs - The Great Train Robber and Nick Leeson, a man who worked on the Stock Market and conned loads of money out of a bank. Some right thugs are here. They make Tara and Katy look like angels – honest they do!

We had netball this morning. One of my new friends, Georgina, is the captain and she picked me to play in her team. Well, when we played Grievous we got loads of cuts and bruises. A horrible girl called Penelope Freestone has got it in for me – wow can she kick! Anyway when Arson played, one of the girls got sent off and she set fire to Miss Asquith's hockey stick! (She's the P.E. teacher – we call her Dairy Box because she's always snacking on chocolate) When all the fuss had died down, I couldn't find my kit. Someone had stolen it, probably someone from Klepto. They would steal the bogies out of your nose if they could.

Oh, we've joined Karate classes – we need to.

DON'T SHOW THIS LETTER TO MUM AND DAD. I'm going to write them now. If you can't read any of the big words ask someone at school.

Missing you already but if you tell anyone I shall deny it.

Tarar Bro, Love Lottie xxx

Dear Mum and Dad

Missing you lots. Seneta and me have made lots of new friends. The food is all right but not as good as yours Mum.

We are in a big bedroom called a dormitory with four other girls. They are nice - you'd like them. Georgina is good fun and quite practical, the twins are sweet (I can't tell them apart) and Natalie wears a brace and likes wild life.

Love you lots. Seneta sends her love too.

Lottie xxxxxxxxxxxxxxxxxxxxxxx

PS. I lost my purse, can you send me some money and some food. Oh and I need some more shorts for PE. The others shrunk in the wash.
PPS. If Josh shows you his letter take no notice it's full of rubbish to make him laugh.

Well I couldn't tell mum what it was really like could I? It *was* like normal school in many ways, but I soon found out we weren't going to learn much. Art was one big paint fight. Mr Brock (we called him Brock the Badger) was obsessed with teaching us how to do portraits of famous people, while most girls preferred to paint each other's faces. His other obsession was signatures. No – not getting autographs but copying them, over and over again!

I told Josh the truth mind you. The girls in Grievous *were* so bad they made Tara and Katy look like angels. You never knew what would happen when you turned a corner, or walked down a corridor on your own! We went to Karate classes with the others from our dorm. As Georgie said, it was the sensible thing to do. I didn't tell Josh about pickpocketting though in Criminology. Honest, that's the perfect truth. Goldfingers told us the story of Oliver Twist and then proceeded to teach us how to pick each other's pockets like the Artful Doger!

I looked across at Seneta, lounging on her bed chewing the end of her biro. I remembered our first day at the school when she stole our purses.

'Maybe we can get Toyah at her own game now and pick her pocket!'

'My mum would kill me!' she said, giggling.

'If Penelope Freestone doesn't do it first!'

Dairy Box came in then munching a packet of Maltesers.

'C'mon Gels,' she said. 'Let's go for a run.' We raced after her following the trail of chocolates she didn't know she was dropping. She ran dead fast, which was probably why she was thin as a rake. She looked like a man from the back as she took us jogging round the fields, which surrounded the school. Her hair was dead short and she had bulging muscles. Most of the girls had bunked off into the woods by the time we got half way round but she didn't seem to notice, or care. So we followed them and found a nice spot to hang out. We found some big juicy blackberries and gorged ourselves silly, getting purple juice all over our hands and faces.

At first it was good fun having no discipline. It was easy doing things like talking in class and being late. The trouble was that it was hard NOT to do some good things as well. Like one day when Miss Goldsmith said:

'Oh dear, I've left my magnifying glass in the staff room. Would anyone be so kind as to fetch it for me please?'

Seneta's hand shot up.

'Stupid girl!' said Goldfingers as her eyes nearly changed places. 'You weren't sent here for being good. It's a little late for that now. Clean up the dining room after dinner! You go Georgina.'

'Why me?' Georgina complained. 'Go yourself!

'That's more like it! Take 20 extra house points. Now run along. It's on the table next to the coffee machine.'

I looked up at a plaque on the wall. On it was written the school motto:

IF YOU ARE GOING TO BE BAD,
YOU MAY AS WELL DO IT PROPERLY.

Crackers or what?

Dinner that evening was the usual messy chaos. After tackling greasy Irish stew and watery rice pudding, I stayed behind with Georgina and Natalie to help Seneta with her punishment. We had to pretend to be hindering her or Miss Orrell, commonly known as Olly the Owl, would have thrown us out. She was on punishment duty. I was a bit scared of her. She looked so strict strutting around with her hands clasped behind her back and peering down her parrot nose at me. I hadn't yet cottoned on to cheeking the teachers. It didn't seem right. Georgie seemed to know what to do. She started drawing graffiti on the wall. Olly walked over and watched her and while her back was turned Natalie picked up a broken plate and pretended to throw it at me. I ducked and it landed in the bin. I did the same and we had cleared up in no time. We pretended to get in Seneta's way while she wiped the tables and Olly seemed to be satisfied.

'What would happen if she caught you helping me?' asked Seneta. 'After all, you're already doing punishment in a way.'

'Clean the toilets I imagine,' was my grim reply.

'Ugh, gross!'

Topsy and Flopsy were in punishment as well. They had been caught watching Blue Peter on telly. They were scraping the leftovers into a huge dustbin and washing up the unbroken pots, not that there were many of those. I looked at the disgusting bin of leftovers and had an idea.

'I know that look on your face,' said Seneta. 'What are you plotting?'

'I'm going to beat Penelope Freestone at her own game.'

*

Sometime later, we were all hiding in the trees near the sports ground. Grievous had been playing netball against Arson and the two teams had been in the shower block for quite a while. There was an oak tree nearby. Mum would have been admiring the red and gold leaves but I was watching something entirely different. Balancing on one of the branches was a large black plastic dustbin.

One or two girls had started to emerge from the brick building looking all pink and shiny. Melanie was one of them. She had a nasty bruise on her shin, which was rapidly turning several shades of purple.

'Who did that to you Melanie?' I whispered as she walked past. She nearly jumped out of her skin.

'I'll give you three guesses,' she said. 'What are you doing here anyway?'

'Stick around and you'll find out.'

Georgina was the first to spot Penelope and she whistled a signal to me.

I came out of my hiding place and shouted.

'How many goals did you score Penny?'

She turned towards me with a face like thunder.

'I'VE TOLD YOU NEVER TO CALL ME PENNY YOU GINGER HAIRED HIPPOPOTAMUS!'

That was good coming from her. I was usually called a stick insect. However I needed her a little nearer.

'It takes one to know one.' Her face went the colour of beetroot as she walked towards me, pushing up her sleeves. Was I supposed to be frightened? I turned my back and walked away. Oh, I forgot to tell you, I was holding on to a piece of string, which was attached to the gloriously smelly, gloriously full dustbin.

I tugged on the invisible line. The bin rocked slowly. I thought it wasn't going to tip and I looked up. Penelope was taken off guard and tilted her head to follow my gaze. I tugged harder. It was such a shame. Penelope had looked so clean and shining before a mixture of rice pudding, Irish stew, jelly and custard came gushing down on top of her and her friends.

'Cool,' said Melanie, as she joined us in high fives.

'Oh my life,' cried Topsy as we legged it as fast as we could.

*

Later, when we were safely in our room and our hysterics had died down, I started to think. We never saw any cleaners. There weren't many teachers either. We hardly ever saw Mrs Potts, the Head Teacher. Mr Potts, a weedy little man with a baldhead was about half her size. He scuttled about with his shoulders hunched and his shifty eyes moving from side to side as if he was at a never-ending tennis match. I had a funny feeling that he was up to something.

'This place stinks,' I said. 'Where are the cleaners?'

'There aren't any, we do it all,' Natalie pointed out.

'So, why do good things get punished and not the other way round?'

'Because bad girls wouldn't do it properly,' Georgie commented, getting quite interested. 'What are you getting at?'

'Suppose there's something funny going on and they don't want cleaners snooping around?'

'Like what?' asked Seneta, becoming interested.

'I don't know. But I do know this. We're never going to learn anything at this rate. We'll all be thickoes by the time we leave school. We'll have to study in our own time.'

'That is *so* not cool!' groaned Seneta.

'I know, I can't believe I'm saying it but all we'll be fit for is a life of crime. You'll never be a nurse at this rate, Seneta. Is that what you want?'

Seneta inspected her fingernails. No one said anything at first. I began to feel like Goody Two Shoes.

'It's not a bad idea, you know.'

Good old Georgie, I knew I could rely on her. The twins shrugged. Flopsy bit her bottom lip.

'How?' Seneta bit off a piece of nail that had escaped earlier inspection. 'We'd get caught if we did it here and we've got no books.'

'We could steal some from the staff library. No one ever goes there,' squeaked Topsy, surprising everyone.

'But you hated lessons, Topsy,' reasoned her sister. 'Have you forgotten?'

Topsy looked upset.

'Why didn't you like lessons Topsy?' I asked, glad that Flopsy had used her name. I still got them mixed up.

'Because I can't read and write properly,' she said, sadly. 'Everything gets back to front.'

'You might be dyslexic,' I told her. 'Have you told anyone?'

She shook her head.

'Oh my life! What will happen to her?' asked Flopsy, looking decidedly worried.

'Nothing,' Georgie pointed out. 'She needs a special sort of help that's all. We'll get some books and find a room at the top of the tower, where we won't be disturbed.'

'I'm not going up there,' said Natalie, shaking her head. 'That's where the White Lady walks.'

Natalie was a dreamer who liked nothing better than to sit on the windowsill watching the birds. She was quiet and didn't say much but when she did, people took notice.

'Who's the White Lady?' Seneta asked.

Georgina explained:

'She's a ghost who walks around at night time, moaning and rattling chains!'

She grabbed a sheet, throwing it over herself.

'Like this! Whooooo!'

'Oh no!' whined Seneta. 'I'm not going up there.'

I sighed and buried my head in my very hard pillow.

Chapter 5 – THE WHITE LADY

I don't really believe in ghosts. Even so, it was with my heart in my mouth that I climbed the stairs that night looking for somewhere to study. Georgina had managed to find a book by Shakespeare, called Anthony and Cleopatra. I found one called History of the World and a World Atlas. Seneta had a Travel Scrabble, which she kindly lent to Topsy along with her own copy of The Secret Garden.

We crept up the creaky stairs. All was quiet, except for the howling wind outside. The old fashioned portraits looked real in the dim light and seemed to be looking down at us with suspicion. Seneta was a bag of nerves and when she said she could hear moaning, I thought it was her imagination.

'Shut up Seneta,' I whispered crossly. 'It's only the wind.'

Natalie, who had only come with us because she didn't want to be left alone in the dormitory, was even worse - if that's possible.

'Oh no - it's the White Lady! I'm off!' she said, attempting to turn back.

'Calm down, Natalie!' I grabbed her arm. 'We're in this together.'

'Oh my life!' whispered Topsy, huddling even more close to her sister than usual.

'Shhhh!'

We crept on up the stairs in silence, trying all the doors but they were locked. It must have looked like a scene from Scooby Doo as we tiptoed on. I looked out of a tall narrow window on the staircase and saw the shape of a bent figure, very much like Mr Potts, coming out of the bushes carrying a large box. I didn't have much time to think about it because suddenly Topsy grabbed my sweatshirt and pointed to a door. There was smoke coming from underneath. We could hear a whimpering and coughing from inside.

'It *is* the White Lady!' said Natalie, terrified of what was inside.

'Shut up Natalie - ghosts don't set fire to things!' Georgina reasoned while trying to open the door. It was no use.

'M-m-maybe it's a P-poltergeist,' Seneta stuttered, most unhelpfully.

'Poltergeists don't cough,' I said, banging on the door. Not that I'd ever met one.

'Open the door!' Georgina shouted to whoever was inside.

Natalie distracted us with a piercing cry. In the moonlight we could see that her face had gone as pale as the moon itself. We followed her gaze and stood, like statues, with our mouths wide open.

A ghostly figure, dressed in white, seemed to be floating down the spiral staircase. She was carrying a large bunch of keys, which rattled as she moved. Natalie fainted on the spot. Dozens of lettered tiles scattered down the staircase like hailstones on a tin roof. Flopsy had dropped the Scrabble.

Georgina was the first to come to her senses.

'It's Miss Lavender!' she said. 'I thought she had died!'

Miss Lavender, whoever she was, took hold of the situation.

'I'm not dead. I'm very much alive, thank you Georgina! Someone help Natalie. Lift her legs up she will soon come round, then fetch her some water. And pick those tiles up before anyone breaks their neck! You girl, fetch that fire extinguisher off the wall over there. I lifted it off the wall and followed her. She opened the door to the smoke filled room with one of the keys on the big key ring. Taking the extinguisher from me she went inside. When she came out, she was carrying Melanie Pearson. They were both coughing. Melanie's face was black.

'She's all right.' said Miss Lavender when she had got her breath. 'It was only a small fire in a waste bin and it's out now.'

She went up the staircase and we followed like lambs. No one said a word. We thought we were in big trouble because she looked so serious. I wondered if we would have to clean the whole school for trying to be good or if Melanie would get ten billion house points for setting fire to it.

Not for the first time, I wished that I were home in Derbyshire eating one of Mum's apple pies. I'd even have given Josh some! When we reached the top of the tower, Miss Lavender opened one of the doors and we all followed her inside. The small room was quite cosy, with a settee and some chairs and a nice pink fluffy rug. There was a stereo in the corner but no TV. She made sure that Natalie and Melanie were both ok and gave us all a drink of fruit juice.

'Now would you mind telling me what you are all up to?' she had a grim look on her pale face. 'Melanie, you first.'

'I like drawing but I get into trouble for doing it. I prefer drawing animals, not those silly portraits of Abraham Lincoln. One night I decided to look for an empty room so that I could draw in peace. I found one and went there every night. Tonight I was cross with myself because I couldn't get a horse's head right, so I burned my drawing. That's why they sent me here, for setting fire to things. I don't know why I do it.

'Well, we'll have to see what we can do about that.' Miss Lavender was writing in a notebook. 'Now, what about the rest of you? Joining the drawing class were we?'

I decided that because it was my idea I had better take the blame.

'It was my fault,' I said. 'I thought we ought to learn something useful for when we get out of here, so we were looking for a room to study in.'

I showed her the books we had borrowed and held my breath, waiting for my punishment. I needn't have worried.

'I think I owe you an explanation now.'

Miss Lavender was quite beautiful, in an older sort of way. She had high cheekbones with fine lines, which made her face look kind like my grannies. She told us how she had had an argument with Mr. Potts about the teaching methods at the school, reverse psychology I think she called it.

'What's that?' asked one of the twins, eyes wide open. Miss Lavender smiled.

'They tell think all children, hmm, young ladies, do the opposite of what they're told to do. I said it was just a lazy way of making money. Mrs Potts sacked me but I had got nowhere to go, so I crept back the same night. I had a spare set of keys (*this explained the rattling*) and I found the attic room, which I made homely with my personal belongings. I only went out at night for something to eat and was content with my stereo (*which explained the music*). But sometimes I would be lonely and cry myself to sleep (*this would be the moaning*). I hoped to get another job but it was difficult without any references to tell anyone that I was a good teacher.'

She couldn't explain the clanking noises when we asked her. Apparently she'd heard them as well.

We visited Miss Lavender regularly after that. She told us about when she was young. Her soldier boyfriend had got killed in Northern Ireland when she was at college. It was so sad. She told us lots of things that happened in the world during her long life – about wars in the Middle East and the Falklands. She showed us where they were on maps. She told us about pop groups, (her favourites were The Rolling Stones) and film stars like Mel Gibson and Kate Winslet. We loved to hear about the Royal Family and when she had camped out in London, in the Mall, to see Prince Charles and Princess Diana's wedding.

More than once Topsy was heard to say:

'Oh my life. How exciting!'

*

Things don't always happen the way you intend. Seneta was my best friend. We told each other everything – all our worries and hopes and dreams. And we had vowed to help each other through this terrible nightmare. We had our differences of course, everyone does. But the last thing I wanted was to fall out with her – it just happened.

Halfway up the stairs on our way to visit Miss Lavender one evening, I was dreaming about Mum's pasta fish bake, when a door opened and Toyah appeared.

'Where are you lot going?' she demanded, screwing her nose up as if there was a bad smell.

'Never you mind, said Georgina. 'It's none of your business!'

'Get back to your room or I'll report you,' Toyah yelled in her bossy prefect manner.

'Then surely we'll get ten thousand extra house points,' Seneta suggested boldly. She hated Toyah as much as I hated Penelope. Toyah was about to blow her top when I had an idea. I decided that the time had come to get even with her for stealing our purses.

'Seneta's right,' I said, folding my arms defiantly. 'If we refuse to go back to our room, *we'll* get extra house points but *you*'ll get into trouble for not doing your job. You'll be stripped of your prefect's badge and everyone will laugh at you. Maybe even Megan Evans will become prefect. You'd like that, wouldn't you?'

Megan Evans was a Welsh girl who thought she was it. And she was as spiteful as Toyah. I knew she was always trying to get one over on Toyah and become prefect herself. Toyah knew it too. Her face fell and I knew I had scored one over on her.

'Go on up girls, while Toyah and I have a nice little chat.'

The girls needed no further bidding and I followed Toyah back into the room. Seneta seemed to hang back but then decided against it and ran after the others. Once inside the room I looked around. It was more like a store cupboard than a room. There were racks of wooden shelves containing cardboard boxes, mostly containing papers. On one of them was written 'Toyah Tranter – PRIVATE – KEEP OUT'. Before she could stop me, I lifted the lid and saw that it contained a collection of different purses, mobile phones and Ipods.

'So this is how prefects behave is it? Stealing things from new girls who are nervous and frightened?' I was prodding her in the chest with my finger and she was backing off.

'Huh, nervous and frightened!' she said, sneering. She brushed her frizzy hair away from her face but it just fell back again. 'Most of them are hard cases; they can look after themselves. When they're not burning the place down they're kicking you in the shins. Anyway they can always get more money from home. Letters and parcels are always arriving for someone but there's never anything for me. Nobody sends me anything, not

55

even my own mother. She's too busy going out with her fancy men and spending her money on new clothes.

My Nan sent me a letter once; I've still got it. She said I could go and live with her. I felt loved. Then she went and died. I didn't know for ages until my fifteenth birthday when my brother, Troy, decided to ring me. And that wasn't to wish me 'Happy Birthday'; I don't think he'd even remembered. He rang to ask if I could lend him some money! *"Where do you think I am, on an oil rig? Go and ask Nan."* I said. 'Do you know what he said?'

I shook my head.

'He said: "I can't, she's dead." Just like that! I was so upset I went and tore up the letter. I felt so cross with her for leaving me.'

She opened another box. There were a few photos in it and some cutouts of pop stars. From underneath a picture of Venus and Serena Williams, the tennis players, she pulled out a letter. It was the one from her Nan. It had been torn into eight pieces and stuck together with sticky tape. Her hands were shaking as she passed it to me.
Dear Toyah, it read.

I hope you are settling in at your new school and also hope you are making new friends. It will do you good to get away from that gang who were such a bad influence on you.

I saw your mum yesterday and she looked luvely in a new purple dress and new shoes. She says she's moved in with her boyfriend Vince and can't remember if she's told you. I said I would write to let you know and she sends her love. She says there's not much room at his place so Troy has gone to stay with a friend. When you come home from school you can come and stay with me. You can have the sofa bed in the living room.

That's all for now, keep doing your learning and you'll get a good job when you leave.

Lots of love from Nan. xxxxx

PS. I can't afford to put any money in because someone pinched my handbag last week when I had just collected my pension. I will send you some next time and you can go to that shop in the village you told me about. God bless!

I handed back the letter. Toyah took it and gently folded it. Before she put it back in the box she gave it a little kiss. Wiping her eyes with the back of her hand she looked at me.

'I've never showed it to anybody before,' she said quietly.

I felt so sorry for her. My mum had always told me that there were two sides to every story. Forgetting my resolve to get even, I decided to take a chance.

'Look,' I said. 'Leave us alone and I'll share my next parcel with you. Mum and Dad are bound to send me one for my birthday in October.'

Toyah stared at me through narrow eyes.

'W ... Why would you do that?' she said. 'What were you all going upstairs for anyway? Ghost hunting?'

'Well ...'

I've never been very good at lying and couldn't make up my mind what to tell her. I decided on the truth.

'We're trying to learn something. We found some books.' I didn't mention Miss Lavender though, just in case.

'Is that all?' She sounded disappointed. 'I'm no good at lessons but I love games. I'd really like to play tennis but they don't do it here. I'd love to go to Wimbledon one day.'

'But there *are* tennis courts round the back of the East Tower,' I reminded her. 'And I'm sure I've seen some old racquets in the games room.'

'Yes I know but who would want to play with me?'

Sitting down, she put her head in her hands. She looked pathetic. It made me wonder what it was like to have no friends.

'I will.'

'You?'

She looked up. Dirty tear-stained streaks ran down her olive coloured cheeks. She smiled and her face looked softer. It was as if no one had ever been kind to her before.

'Well ok, but don't tell anybody about me crying an all that, or else you're dead!'

I agreed but wondered what I'd done. And how was I going to tell Seneta?

Chapter 6 – THE QUARREL

'How could you!' shouted Seneta when I told her later. 'She stole our money! *And* playing tennis with her – she's a chav! She's too old anyway. I thought you were *my* friend.'

'I am but I can have other friends as well can't I? And she's only 15 not 50. Anyway it's better to have a prefect on our side than against us.'

'Other friends? Ha. Toyah's not a friend, she's a project. Lottie Longfellow, Saviour of the World, don't make me sick. You risked everything for that … that …

'That what, Seneta?'

'That thieving blob! You know I want to get on and be a nurse. How did you know it wasn't a trick? And what about Miss Lavender? She could lose her home if Toyah tells on her.'

'I didn't mention Miss Lavender.'

'So what is it then? Are you jealous of me being in the Centre of Excellence? Is that what it is? Did you purposely try to put a stop to our studies?

'Jealous? Of *you*? Don't make me laugh. And why would I do that? I suggested it in the first place. You – you - you. That's all you think about – yourself! Other people have hopes and dreams as well you know.'

'What hopes and dreams have you got then. I thought so – none.'

'At least I've got a mind of my own. You only want to be a nurse because your mum is one!

You're not cut out to be a nurse. Nurses are supposed to be kind not spiteful.'

'You just want to spoil everything for me. We wouldn't be here if it wasn't for you. Anyway Miss Lavender said she would help me get qualifications to be a nurse.'

'You can be a brain surgeon for all I care – and practice on yourself!'

With that I grabbed my towel and marched off to the bathroom, slamming the door behind me.

Don't you say some awful things when you're angry? The trouble was I didn't know why I was angry. I thought Seneta would understand about Toyah. I wasn't jealous of her, not really. But I was worried about the extra lessons she had been attending. The Centre of Excellence for Natural Talent they called it, CENT for short.

Seneta was good at art as well as Melanie but, whereas Melanie was good at portraits and animals, Seneta was ace at drawing intricate patterns, fine art I think she called it. It was because of this that she attended CENT with some other gifted girls, which was fine by me. But what was the point in a school, which didn't seem to care about anything?

There was Melanie and Erin Jones from Arson, Ellie Worthington from Klepto and, oh yes, Natasha Shipman. I think she was from Klepto as well. Surprise, surprise, there was no one from Grievous.

Another puzzling thing was that none of them talked about it. When you asked anyone what happened there, they just said 'Oh nothing much, I can't remember.' If I asked Seneta, she got cross and accused me of being jealous. It was as if they'd joined a secret society. Suddenly, at any time of day, they would all stop what they were doing and walk off. I tried following them once but they seemed to disappear into thin air. And if it was such a good thing, why weren't they punished? Teachers kept telling us it was too late to be good and then they start rewarding *talent*; I couldn't understand it at all.

I went to the bathroom to have a shower and clean my teeth. I felt homesick and wished I had my mum to talk to. This place was getting to me. It turned everything topsy turvey. Seneta and I had never argued before.

When I got back to the dormatory, the door was slightly open. The others had returned and I could hear them talking. I stood outside listening.

'She could have got us all into trouble,' Georgina said as she snapped her glasses case shut. 'And are you saying she lied to us; that you were sent here for being bullies?'

I gasped but couldn't see Seneta through the crack in the door. I did see the twins folding up their clothes. They dived into bed in their banana yellow pj's.

'Oh my life!' said Topsy. 'I don't like that Toyah.'

'Nor me,' agreed her sister.

'I wish you'd all stop whithpering,' moaned Natalie as she brushed her long hair. 'I can't hear you.'

'We were saying that Lottie had no right to tell Toyah about our lessons,' Georgina said loudly. And she should really be in Grievous.'

'Oh. I don't believe that. It must be a mithtake, right Seneta?'

Good old Natalie! At least someone stuck up for me.

'Yes well she's had it now,' said Seneta. 'I'm never going to speak to her again! You won't throw me out will you? I'm not a bully.'

'We won't throw either of you out,' Georgina assured her, not sounding happy at all.

I walked in and they all went quiet. I apologised for lying to them and told them all about Tara and Katy. All the while I looked to my snitch of a friend to help me out. She was in bed and remained facing the wall.

'Please understand Seneta. Toyah is lonely. She needs a friend.'

'Go and be friends with that racist pig then but don't expect to be friends with me. As far as I'm concerned you're just as bad as her.'

Seneta pulled the covers over her head as if to say – discussion over.

I climbed into bed with a heavy heart and couldn't help but notice how quiet the room was.

CHAPTER 7 – BIRTHDAY GIRL

I had been under a black cloud for days. Seneta still wasn't speaking to me. I thought she was being a bit childish but I would have done anything to get back with her – except upset Toyah. I know she had a big mouth and everybody hated her but she was quite different when we were alone – softer, friendlier, more human. It was difficult for the other girls in the dorm though. They were ok with me when Seneta wasn't around but there was a horrible atmosphere when she was. Georgina was great; she kept drawing us both into the conversation, pretending that there was nothing wrong.

'I can't say that I like that Toyah very much,' she confided in me one day. 'But I respect your reasons for befriending her. After all we all need someone. I don't know what I would have done without Nat. Anyway, I think Seneta will need you before you need her.'

That didn't make me feel any better. I knew Seneta would be too proud to make the first move. There had to be another way.

*

Toyah and I had found some old racquets in the sports cupboard. One had a string missing but it was useable and we had some fun. Toyah turned out to be quite good. Her backhand smash was very powerful and she beat me most times.

We arrived at the showers one morning after a game, which seemed to go on forever and, because I was bursting to go to the loo, we called it a draw.

'Did you see fish-face at breakfast?' Toyah said in a loud voice while she was showering. 'I'm sure she was drunk!'

I *had* seen Miss Haddock putting a fried egg on top of a Weetabix but the school was so weird, I wasn't surprised at anything any more.

'Yes I did – what a weirdo.' I looked at Toyah as she came out of the shower, dripping and shivering. 'Tell you something I bet you didn't know. All this exercise is making you slimmer.'

*

At 8 o'clock on 15th October there was a knock on our dormitory door. Toyah pushed a parcel into my hands.

'This came for you.'

I was just about to thank her but the door slammed in my face. I turned to look at Seneta and couldn't help noticing a smirk before she showed me her back. Wondering what was up with Toyah, I opened the parcel. Inside was a pretty card from my Mum and Dad with some money inside. They also sent me a lovely cake, covered with pink roses and *Happy Birthday Lottie* written in pink icing. There were some of my favourite chocolates in a pyramid shaped box and a beaded box containing nail varnish, hair clips and hair gel, which I really needed. Josh sent me a wildlife poster of some polar bears and a card, which had *Teenager* on the front.

The next person to knock on the door was Melanie, bringing me a card she had made herself.

On it she had drawn a beautiful picture of a horse and a foal, which she had copied from a book.

'I'll keep it forever,' I said. 'And when you're a famous artist, it will be worth a fortune.'

Melanie grinned proudly.

I cut the cake and offered it round but when I got to Seneta she closed her eyes and went out. Biting my bottom lip, I watched her go - wishing things were different. However I was soon showered with cards and presents. The twins got me a silver dolphin on a black cord to hand round my neck. Georgina and Natalie gave me some shower gel and hand cream. They were lovely but I would have traded them all for a card from Seneta.

Wearing my new hair clips, I met Toyah in the television room and gave her a chocolate and a slice of cake.

'Happy Birthday,' she said, handing me a card. She had made it herself by cutting a picture of two Scottie dogs from a magazine.

'Thanks, I love dogs,' I said, studying the card. 'What was up with you earlier?'

She shrugged her shoulders. It seemed that I was the only one who was allowed to see the nice side of her.

'I've got you a present!' she announced as a big smile spread across her face and two pink patches invaded her cheeks. She was excited about something!

I looked round the room but I couldn't see anything wrapped in pretty paper. Suddenly I had an awful thought.

'You've not been stealing again have you?'

'No!' she snapped and marched outside in a strop.

I followed. It was still quite early and a cool breeze ran over me. I shivered, wishing I had put my coat on but didn't say anything. Better not spoil her moment. I wondered what it was and followed her down a path into the woods. I hadn't been that way before. She was walking so fast I could hardly keep up. We reached a sort of farmyard. I saw some old stables. To my surprise, a door flew open and out staggered Mr Potts! He tried to stand still when he saw us.

'Good morning Mr Potts.' We both tried to act normally.

'Er, good morning girls,' he answered. 'Where are you going?'

'For a walk, sir.'

Toyah pointed down another path. Mr Potts's eyes darted from side to side as if he'd forgotten what he was doing.

'Carry on then!' he said.

I could hear a tap, tap, tap. It reminded me of the way Mrs Potts tapped on the desk with her painted nails. I glanced back at the stables, wondering what was going on in there. Was it anything to do with the Centre of Excellence for Natural Talent? Whatever it was, I was sure there was something odd about Mr Potts. He stood unsteadily and watched us walk away. I resolved to come back another time and investigate

Reaching a clearing in the trees we came across an old potting shed. The door was locked with a big rusty padlock but Toyah went round the back and removed a loose piece of wood. We both crawled inside. This is the surprise, I thought. Toyah has found a den!

It was quite dark as I climbed through the hole, only to be set upon by a wild animal, all sharp claws, slavering mouth and growls. I screamed.

'It's ok Lottie,' said Toyah, laughing. 'Get down, Scruffy!'

I tried to get up but was smothered by a big rough wet tongue.

'She's saying Happy Birthday,' said Toyah in fits of giggles.

'What is it? I said as my eyes got used to the gloom.

'It's a dog, silly! Well a bitch to be accurate – that's not swearing – it means girl dog. I found her on the road. She was exhausted. Some creep had dumped her out of a car and she must have kept running until she couldn't run any more. I don't know how people can be so cruel.'

'She's skinny!'

'I know but we can feed her and take her for walks.'

'This is my present?'

'Don't you like her?'

I looked at the dog. She was extremely thin and didn't smell very pleasant. Her shaggy coat appeared to be black and white but it was difficult to tell, she was so dirty! The fur on her head fell forward like a fringe, which reminded me of Cleopatra, an Egyptian queen Miss Lavender had been telling us about. She was looking at me with her head on one side. Her tongue was hanging out of the side of her mouth and saliva was dripping on the floor. She was panting like an old tractor and had a pleading expression in her sorrowful eyes. I looked at Toyah. She had the same pleading expression.

'Well?' she urged.

'How will I look after her?'

'She can stay here. She won't mind. We can take her for walks and we can sneak leftovers out for her – there is always plenty. Go on - say you'll keep her.'

'Ok. I'll call her Cleo,' I said, giving them both a hug. 'Thanks Toyah! I don't know how we're going to pull it off but it's the best present I've ever had!

*

'Gosh! What happened to you two? You're wet through.'

'It was my birthday present, Georgie'

'Well, I know I bought you bubble bath but you're supposed to take your clothes off!'

'No, not *your* present Georgie – Toyah's.'

Toyah looked sulky because I'd told our secret.

'Go on then, tell her!' she said, with a sigh.

'No, we'll show her,' I told her, excitedly.

We took her to the shed where we had left Cleo and climbed through the secret hole. Cleo jumped up and licked each one of us in turn, knocking us over in the process. She smelled of damp dog but she was a lot cleaner.

'Georgie meet Cleo!' I said.

'She's gorgeous! Where did you get her? What a present! She makes my bubble bath look a bit sick,' Georgina gabbled, as she fussed Cleo.

'I found her,' said Toyah, proudly. 'And we dunked her in an old horse trough that was filled with rainwater.'

'And I love your present,' I added. 'I'm going to need plenty of bubble bath when this four legged bundle of fur has finished with me. At least you smell a bit sweeter now, don't you Cleo?'

I patted the dog. She took this as another invitation for cuddles and jumped on me, smothering my face with slimy licks. I couldn't get up for laughing. Suddenly we heard a shout from outside. We looked out through the cobwebby window and saw Penelope Freestone and company chasing the twins and catching up fast. Flopsy screamed as Penelope got hold of her.

'Oh my life, let her go,' squealed Topsy.

I don't know if it was the noise that scared Cleo but she went mad. As soon as Toyah lifted up the wooden board for us to get out and help our friends, she shot through the hole like a bullet. The last we saw, she was careering into the bushes.

'Well, well, well!'

Penelope and the other two stopped in their tracks as we crawled through the hole.

'What do we have here? She was still holding Flopsy by the ear. 'Sucking up to prefects now are we? Where did that mangy mutt come from?'

'None of your business and leave those girls alone Penny!' I retorted, shortening her name on purpose.'

'Why you, you ....'

She pushed Flopsy to one side and turned her attention to me.

'Run twins!' I shouted, grabbing Penelope's hair so that she couldn't follow.

Georgina and Toyah got stuck into Deirdre and Tina, who soon scuttled away like the cowards they were. Penelope clawed at my face like a wild animal, causing me to yell out in pain and let go. She grabbed hold of my neck and pushed me to the floor. I got hold of her leg as she was about to kick me but she managed to pull it free. Toyah and Georgie came to my rescue just as she scrunched her size seven Doc Martin boot into my face. All of a sudden, she turned into a whimpering, snivelling, wreck, begging us not to hurt her.

We let her go threatening to come after her if she chased the twins again. She ran after her friends.

'Wait till I get you, Tina Feathers! Call yourself a friend, Deirdre Richardson? You might well hide!'

'Are you all right?' Georgina asked me.

'I've felt better! But where is Cleo?'

We searched the woods, calling her name but we couldn't find her. Toyah and I were frantic.

'Don't worry, she probably doesn't know her new name yet.' said Georgina, trying to cheer us up. 'Did you give her anything to eat?'

'I brought her some burnt toast with peanut butter,' said Toyah.

'Then she'll come back,' said Georgina. 'Let's go into the village and get her some proper dog food. Have you got any money?'

I nodded.

'I had some for my birthday.'

I tried to smile but my mouth hurt.

'I've got to go back and do some prefecting,' said Toyah, miserably.

'You mean you have to dish out more chores to innocent girls,' Georgina said, grimacing.

Toyah looked ashamed.

'Sort of; I'll see you later.'

'Well, don't forget to start on Penelope, Tina and Deirdre.'

'Ok, no probs.'

Georgina watched her go and surprised me by saying:

'She's not so bad is she?'

BAD SCHOOL

Chapter 8 - WINNIE

The nearest village to school was Grimstone. By road, it was about three miles but we took a short cut across a farm. It had been raining hard recently and, where the cows came in for milking, it was as muddy as Glastonbury.

'It stinks here, but it's a lot quicker than going by road,' observed Georgie, holding her nose.

I wasn't so sure as my feet slipped and slithered in the gloopy mess. Eventually we arrived at the shop; shoes caked in mud. Georgina got to the door first.

'Oh no!'

'What's up?'

'This!'

There was a note on the door:

NO GIRLS FROM GRIMSTONE PRIORY ALLOWED IN THIS SHOP - BY ORDER OF THE MANAGEMENT.

'I bet those girls from Klepto have been pilfering again,' said Georgina, in disgust. 'We all get tarred with the same brush. It's not fair.'

The shop door opened with a 'ding' and a little old lady came struggling out with a shopping trolley. She had grey permed hair, and she had an old brown coat on. Her hands were a funny shape and there were bumps on her fingers. Georgie held the door for her and I lifted the trolley and helped her down the step.

'Thank you girls, that's very kind of you. Are you going in?' she asked.

'We're not allowed.' I pointed to the note on the door. But we need some things for our new dog.'

I showed her my list:

> 1 large bag dried dog food
> 1 collar and lead for medium sized dog
> Dog shampoo
> 2 bowls
> Brush
> Treats
> Poo bags

She tapped on the door with her brolly. An Indian gentleman came out. The lady poked her bony finger at his chest.

'These girls have a list of things to buy for their dog. They've helped me down the step, so they can't be all that bad. Please serve them or I'll take my business elsewhere!'

Her false teeth went up and down as she talked. I wanted to giggle but I managed to keep a straight face.

The man looked from her to us, and his gaze swept down to our muddy shoes. He took our list and our money.

'Wait there!' he said, sharply.

When he returned with a carrier bag full of doggy things and not much change, the lady said:

Would you like to come to my house for a cup of tea? You look as though you could do with one. It's just down the road.'

Would we like a cup of tea? In a real house? It sounded like heaven. What a nice birthday treat!

'Yes please!'

We reached a row of tiny cottages. They were painted white and looked like dolls houses. Once inside the black front door we took off our muddy shoes. The tiny room was homely and there was a real fire in the grate.

'My name is Winnie Foster,' she said. 'You can call me Winnie, if you like.'

'This is Georgie and I'm Lottie. It's my birthday.' I told her. 'I'm thirteen.'

She plonked herself down in the only armchair and paused to get her breath.

'Well, Happy Birthday teenager! Now Georgie and Lottie, put the kettle on there's good girls.'

We went into the tiny kitchen. There was a sink full of pots and we pulled faces at one another. We thought we had escaped chores, but we washed them up and made some tea.

'There are some scones in the tin and some butter in my shopping basket,' she called. 'Oh and some homemade damson jam in the cupboard.'

We sat on a handmade rag rug in front of the fire, eating jam-dripping scones and drinking hot tea. Her two tabby cats, Sammy and Tiger, curled up with us. It was so warm and cosy I could have stayed there forever. She told us about some of the people in the village. People like Hattie Chislewick, who stole clothes off people's washing lines, and Jim Popplewell, who swept chimneys and came round on New Year's Eve – first footing she called it. Her teeth clicked all the time she was talking and her poor fingers could hardly hold her cup and saucer.

'It's time we were getting back,' said Georgina reluctantly. 'Before someone misses us.'

We said our goodbye, but not before washing our cups and fetching some coal in for her. She said we could come back again any time and bring the dog. We promised we would, if we ever found her.

'I thought her teeth were going to fall out!' said Georgina as Winnie waved to us from the doorstep.

*

I couldn't concentrate on Art that afternoon, what with worrying about Cleo and Seneta. My mind was all mixed up. I dearly wanted to be clever so that I would be invited into CENT. I had to find out what was going on. Mind you, I didn't really expect to excel in Brock the Badger's class. He hated me and took pleasure in making my life difficult.

I was fed up with trying to copy people's names. I was wishing I was at karate instead. Chopper Su was good fun for someone who couldn't speak a word of English. It was a good job it wasn't karate - my partner wouldn't have stood a chance with the mood I was in. As it was, I couldn't see the reason for writing the same name over and over. I'd never even heard of the fellow but his signature was on a copy of a ten-pound note. I tried to draw Cleo from memory. Brock the Badger caught me but, instead of giving me house points, he said:

'Whose signature is that - Lassie? Signatures girl, signatures!' He stood over me, making me do them long after everyone else had gone. I'd never heard of the fellow anyway. Someone called Merlyn Lowther.

'Hopeless girl, hopeless!' he scolded after my zillionth attempt. 'You'll never be any good. No good at all.'

I'd had enough. Throwing down my pen I ran out of the classroom and carried on running until I reached the stables. I sat on a fallen tree and sobbed. This was my birthday. I wanted my mum and dad – and I longed to see the cheeky grin on my disgusting little brother's face.

Its all Seneta's fault not mine I thought. Little thanks I get for trying to help people, ending up in a bad girls' school. Best friend – hah, what a joke that is. She said Toyah was a project but it's not true. I'm not that clever. I'm ordinary - so ordinary that no one notices me. That's why I have spiky hair to make me look different. Seneta knows that - she's a bitch. But Cleo is a bitch and she's lovely. Ok, so Seneta is a cow. But cows have beautiful big brown eyes. Come to think of it, so has Seneta. I ended up adding her to my list of people I miss, even though I saw her every day and she still slept in the bed next to mine.

I wasn't sure if I'd heard right at first. I listened again. Yes there it was again – a faint whimper. It was coming from the stables. I got up and tried the doors but they were all locked. However, stables door split into two, so that the horses can put their heads out. One of the upper doors was unlocked. I pushed it open and climbed in. It was dark and there was a funny smell. I felt around until I found a light switch and clicked it on.

'Cleo!'

She was in the corner, on a pile of papers. She tried to get up when she saw me but, after a wobbly attempt, she fell to the floor.

'Oh Cleo, are you ill?'

I wrapped my arms around her and looked round, wondering what to do. The stables were kitted out like a laboratory. There was a strange contraption, made up of jars and tubes. On some shelves were some jugs and loads of bottles. There were more on the floor, but these had been tipped over. The cork had come out of one of them spilling the contents all over the floor. Cleo must have knocked it over. I dipped my finger into the spilled liquid and tasted it.

'You're drunk!' I said in amazement. She lifted her head to look at me but her eyes met in the middle. She tried to lick me but her tongue fell to one side. I attempted to lift her but she was too heavy, so I went outside to look for someone to help.

I avoided some girls who were smoking and drinking something from cans and took another path. Who should come by but Georgie, jogging round the path, keeping out of sight of slimy prefects!

'Georgie, I've found Cleo!' I shouted.

'Where was she?'

'You'll never guess!'

I told her about the stables and she came with me to help. We carried Cleo between us in Georgie's sports towel. She didn't wake up at all and she was as heavy as a baby elephant!

'Of course, you know what all that stuff was don't you?' Georgina said knowingly.

'I'm not sure.'

'It's a still. To make whisky! That stuff in the bottles is called Moonshine!   My granddad told me all about it. It's terrible stuff – it rots your guts. It must belong to Mr Potts. No wonder he's always looking furtive. Maybe it would be just as well if we didn't tell anyone about this. I agreed and we tucked Cleo up to sleep it off, leaving some water and food for when she woke up.

'I wonder will she have a hangover?' I asked Georgina, as we walked back to school.

'My mum used to say her head felt like it was full of brick's when she'd been drinking. She drank a lot when they split.' Georgina went quiet and looked sad.

'What's it like, when your parents split up?'

'It's awful at first but you get used to it. I see both of them when I go home for the holidays, but not together. Mum's got a boyfriend, Dan, who makes me laugh but I don't like Sally-Ann very much.'

'Is that your dad's girl friend?'

'Yes. She's a lot younger than Dad and is always painting her nails and doing her hair. She doesn't like me being around and is horrible when he's not looking.'

I thought about *my* mum and dad. They always used to talk about the news and stuff. They went on visits to the theatre and country walks. They liked the same things, or used to.

'Perhaps they get on well together.'

'Oh *I* don't know. She seems to be on another planet. They went to London one weekend and when they came back, I asked her if they had seen Cleopatra's Needle. Do you know what she said?'

I shook my head.

'She said she didn't know Cleopatra had lost one!'

I laughed but would have liked to ask her more. I'd been worried about my Mum and Dad for a long time. They had been rowing a lot before I left - being away from them made me worry even more.

However, we had reached the school and as soon as we walked in, we bumped into Toyah and another prefect, called Victoria Garfield. She was from Grievous and built like a Russian shot-putter.

'What have you two been up to? Did you find your friend?' asked Toyah, cheerfully.

I knew she meant Cleo. She was talking in code so that Atilla the Hun wouldn't notice.

'Oh yes thanks. She's gone to bed,' I answered, going along with the code.

I thought it better to steer the conversation away.

'We met a lovely old lady in the village this morning. She invited us to her house and gave us tea and scones. They were scrummy.'

Georgina was quick to catch on.

'Yes, but we had to wash the pots didn't we, Lottie?'

Atilla the Hun scowled.

'Doing good deeds eh? We were looking for someone to clean the toilets, weren't we Toyah?'

Toyah blushed. She didn't know what to say.

'Oh yes, er …'

'But it's tea time!'

Victoria was triumphant.

'Not for you, Ginger. You do the loos in Grievous and you, four-eyes, do the Klepto ones. Properly mind – we'll inspect later.'

'But it's my birthday!'

'Happy Birthday loser,' she said as she shoved a box of cleaning stuff in my face. She took the other box from an embarrassed Toyah and handed it to Georgina.

'You're getting soft,' she said to Toyah, as they walked away. Toyah turned to look at us and shrugged an apology.

'You and your big mouth,' I hissed at Georgina.

'You started it,' she hissed back.

After much scrubbing and polishing, I looked round the room. The toilets were spotless. All seats were down, new toilet rolls in place, bins emptied, mirrors polished and floor mopped. I felt really lucky. Why? Because no one had interrupted me and, believe me, in Grievous toilets that *was* lucky!

I got back to the dormitory but it was empty. I presumed the others had gone up to Miss Lavender's room, so I lay down on my bed for a five-minute rest. Looking across, I saw that Seneta had left her mobile phone on her bedside table. What I'd give for one of those I thought. It would be lovely to ring Mum, Dad and Josh. Mum couldn't afford to get me one when I came away. She said if I were good, maybe I'd get one for Christmas. But that was no good. I needed to talk to them now.

I went over to her bed. The bedside drawer was slightly open and I could see a sketch inside. I slid the drawer open a little wider. There was a pencil drawing of an elephant and the word 'Happy' – beautifully inscribed.

So, I thought. She *was* going to give me a birthday card but she hadn't finished it. I felt a rush of happiness. She did still like me after all. That did it. I knew the old Seneta wouldn't mind me using her phone.

I picked it up and looked at it for a long time. It wasn't one of those you had to top up with money. I knew her mum and dad paid a bill for it every month. She'd never know. And if she found out, she wouldn't mind – not on my birthday. I had talked myself into it. With shaky fingers I pressed in the number. A sweet little voice answered.

'Hello?'

'Hi Turnip Face!'

'Lottie – it's you! Happy Birthday!'

I thanked Josh for the poster and asked what he'd had for tea. I knew before he answered that it was lasagne - it was Thursday for goodness sake. He said he was going to stay with Gran for a few days. Before I could ask him why, Mum took the phone from him. She wished me Happy Birthday, asked me if I'd had a good day and had I received the parcel. I told her about all my presents, missing out the one from Toyah. It was hard to talk on account of the lump in my throat. I mentioned Winnie and the scones, telling her they weren't as good as hers. She said she loved me and asked if I was getting enough to eat. That reminded me that I had missed my tea.

'Too much,' I said, thinking about burnt toast and lumpy porridge. 'Is Dad there?' He came on the phone:

'Hi Pumpkin! Happy Birthday! How are you and how's Seneta? I gather she's lent you her phone.'

Talk of the devil - I could hear footsteps in the corridor!

'Yes, but I've got to go now Dad.'

'Did you get the parcel?'

'Oh yes, it was great thanks. But I've got to go Dad.'

'Did you get the money?'

'Yes thanks, but I need some more. It's terribly expensive round here – you have to pay for everything.'

'Such as what?'

'Everything. Bye Dad! Love you!'

'WHAT DO YOU THINK YOU ARE DOING WITH THAT?'

Seneta was not pleased.

'Oh Seneta, I'm sorry. I thought you wouldn't mind.'

'AND WHY WOULD YOU THINK THAT?'

'You left your drawer open. I saw the card you were making me. Oh Sen ...'

'GET BACK TO YOUR FRIENDS FROM KLEPTO,' she said. 'YOU'RE TURNING INTO ONE OF THEM ALREADY.'

'But Seneta, the card?'

'I'm making the card for my parents. It's a DIVALI card. GET OUT!'

I shivered. The room had gone cold, and it wasn't from the wind whistling round the old window frames. With a heavy heart, I climbed the spiral staircase. What a day it had been! - Full of ups and downs. If only Seneta hadn't come back when she did, it would have finished happily. I knocked on the door of Miss Lavender's room and walked in.

'HAPPY BIRTHDAY!'

Georgina, Natalie, Topsy, Flopsy and Melanie were all there. The table was laid out with sandwiches and crisps. There were sausages on sticks and little cubes of cheese. For afters there was a big trifle and some cream cakes.

'We've been waiting ages for you,' moaned Topsy.

'*I* stuck the sticks in the sausages,' said Flopsy, proudly.

'Georgie and I were supposed to do the sandwiches,' said Natalie. 'But she didn't turn up till it was done.'

Georgina looked at me and grinned.

'Any trouble?'

I shook my head.

'We've even got some music,' interrupted Natalie, as if she hadn't heard what we had said.

'And we're going to watch Grease on video,' said Topsy, excitedly. 'What more could you want?'

Seneta's face and Mum's lasagne came into my head.

'Nothing,' I said. 'It's great. Thanks!'

Miss Lavender smiled.

'It's a pity Seneta couldn't make it,' she said, thoughtfully. 'Such a serious girl… That Centre of Excellence has a lot to answer for.'

'What do you mean Miss Lavender?'

'Oh nothing. Just an old woman's ramblings.'

Georgina interrupted.

'Come on Lottie. You've got to start first and we're hungry,'

'I'll talk to you another time, Lottie,' Miss Lavender whispered. 'Come on, let's party – and don't look so worried!'

Chapter 9 – DIVALI

The next morning in the dorm, Georgie and I were singing I'm the One That You Want while the twins related the story about their run-in with Penelope. Natalie was studying something crawly in a cardboard box.

'Where did the dog come from?' she asked.

'Toyah found her abandoned by cruel owners,' I explained. 'And she gave her to me for a birthday present.'

Natalie became interested.

'Are you going to keep her?'

'I don't see why not.'

Seneta looked up from the book she was reading.

'That's the stupidest thing I've ever heard. How are you going to look after a dog? I bet she stole it. It will be back with its owners by now.'

'No *she* won't,' I replied, secretly pleased that Seneta had said something to me, even if it was horrible. 'Would you like to come and look at her?'

'No I would not. I've got better things to do.'

'Oh well, it's your loss!'

'Can we come, please?' said Topsy.

'If you want to; what about you two?'

'Try and stop me,' said Natalie, linking arms with me.

'Count me in,' agreed Georgina. 'Although I can't work out if it would be house points or chores if we got caught walking a dog.'

'Oh my life,' cried Flopsy.

*

Thankfully, Cleo had recovered from her drunken stupor. The girls thought she was cute. We walked her round the woods, taking it in turns to hold the lead. There was an awkward moment when Toyah appeared but the girls accepted that she had found Cleo so she had a right.

'So long as she keeps her hands in her pockets,' Natalie whispered behind her hand.

Toyah heard and she stuck her out tongue. The sun glinted on Natalie's brace as she grinned.

'I've got to go soon. Miss Lavender has made me an appointment at the doctor's surgery, to check my hearing.'

'That's good Nat,' I said.

Georgina agreed.

'I'll come with you, and the others can visit Winnie while they're waiting.'

When Winnie opened the door, she put her hands to her mouth as if she was holding her loose teeth in.

'Goodness gracious! Is this the whole school? It's a good job I've made another batch of scones.'

She tried to remember our names, but kept getting them mixed up. She remembered Natalie, probably because of the brace but called me Cleo. Georgie became Lottie and she didn't even try with Topsy and Flopsy calling them both 'the twins'. They didn't mind – they were having too much fun playing with Cleo and the cats. All the time, Winnie's teeth clicked away. Toyah thought it was hilarious and couldn't stop giggling. At least she sat behind the settee with her fist stuffed into her mouth.

Georgie and Nat left for the doctors and I dug my teeth into another jammy scone.

'Seneta would love this.'

'Who's Seneta?' Winnie asked. 'The name sounds foreign.'

'She's Indian and she's my best friend,' I said, forgetting Toyah was there. 'The trouble is that we've quarrelled. I would do anything to make up.'

'Why don't you get her a Divali card?' Winnie advised. 'They've got them at the shop. It's their Harvest Festival I believe. Would you like me to get you one?'

'Yes please! What a good idea!'

'What's Divali?' asked Topsy.

'Seneta once told me it was the Festival of Light.' I explained. 'It's like our Christmas with lights and decorations. They go to the Temple and have parties. She will be sad to be away from home.' I remembered the card she had been making for her parents.'

We cleared away the pots. There was a netball match at 11 o'clock so we couldn't stay much longer. Topsy asked if there was anything else we could do before we left. Toyah, who had not helped at all, remembered her prefect duties.

'You're not supposed to be good. Remember? I could give punishment out for this.'

I was disappointed.

'Toyah, don't be like that, please. This is different.'

Winnie looked at Toyah in disbelief.

'Do I understand that you punish girls for being good?'

'Yes. It's the rules of the school.'

'And why do *you* dish out the punishment?'

'Because I'm a prefect - it's my job.'

'Then you are just doing your job?'

'Yes,' she said, smugly.

'So *you* are being good, by doing your job!'

We stood looking from Winnie to Toyah in amazement. Toyah was not pleased. A dark look came over her face and she marched out of the house, slamming the front door behind her.

'Good one Winnie,' I said but inwardly I wasn't so sure. Toyah in a mood was like an out of control firework. Sparks would fly.

'She's a mixed up kid,' Winnie observed and I had to agree.

All of a sudden we heard snoring. Cleo was sprawled on the rug in front of the fire. Cuddled up to her were two tabby cats, and next to them were Topsy and Flopsy. They were all fast asleep! We had to wake them up when the girls came back from the doctors because Georgie and I had promised Dairy Box Asquith we'd play netball. We weren't looking forward to it though because we were playing against Grievous!

As we waved goodbye, I thought I heard a rustle in the bushes nearby. I turned and imagined I saw someone hide behind a brick wall but when I looked there was nobody there.

'C'mon,' urged Georgie. 'We're late.'

*

We lost the netball match 43-2. After we had dabbed our bruises with witch hazel we had some cheese rolls and soup. I don't know what flavour the soup was but I'm sure the cheese was galvanised rubber. After lunch the others went to Maths but I snook off to see Miss Lavender.

'Thank you for the party,' I said, when she greeted me. 'As my little brother would say, it was well good.'

'You're very welcome,' she said. 'You girls have given me a new lease of life. Now - about Seneta?

'What did you mean, when you said that the Centre of Excellence has a lot to answer for?' I asked.

'Well, nothing that I can put my finger on, but Melanie and Seneta seem to be in a trance most of the time.'

'And Seneta gets so cross. We've never argued much before and when we did, we soon made up. We were inseparable.'

'I see. So Seneta is acting quite out of character?'

'Yes.'

'I think I need to write a letter,' she said, mysteriously. 'And it's long overdue.'

She wouldn't say anymore, so I told her about my idea. She thought it was brilliant and we made plans.

*

A couple of days later, Natalie had to go to the hospital to have a hearing aid fitted. She asked Seneta to go with her. Georgie didn't mind at all because it was part of the plan. Miss Lavender told Natalie that she might find the new equipment a bit strange and the noise of the dining room might upset her. She offered to cook a meal to celebrate. Seneta went along with this, and didn't suspect a thing!

While they were at the hospital, I helped Georgie and Miss Lavender to prepare the food. Topsy and Flopsy made garlands and Melanie wrote out a verse in her beautiful handwriting.

We were hanging some Christmas lights round the room when Topsy shouted:

'They're coming up the drive.'

That gave us time to light the tea candles, switch on the fairy lights and switch the main light off. We had done a wonderful job, I don't mind telling you. It looked so romantic in the flickering candlelight. When Seneta appeared with Natalie we all shouted: HAPPY DIVALI!' She beamed with pleasure.

'Before we start Seneta, I want you to know this was all Lottie's idea,' Miss Lavender said. Seneta looked at me and I smiled. 'Now, come with me,' she continued, and took her into the bedroom. When she came out we gasped. Miss Lavender had dressed her in a sari. I don't know where it came from. It was purple silk and was wrapped round and round her. Her head was covered in beautiful lace decorated with beads, and she had a pink mark on her forehead. She looked amazing.

Topsy carefully read out the words to the Hindu national anthem – Thou Art the Ruler of Minds. It was very difficult for her and we all cheered.

I gave Seneta my card. It had a picture of the Elephant God, Ganesh, on the front. He was a fat man with four arms and a potbelly. He had an elephant's head with a single tusk.

Seneta looked at me with tears in her eyes.

'Thank you,' she said. I was dead chuffed and wished Winnie could be there to see her.

'Come along then,' said Miss Lavender. 'Let's tuck in. Seneta - you first!'

There was pilau rice and samosas, spring rolls and onion barjis, with lots of lemonade to wash it all down. It was really spicy but I liked the flavours. It reminded me of eating at Seneta's house. It seemed so long ago. Natalie was happy with her hearing aid; she said she could even hear the prawn crackers crunching! Miss Lavender had found a record of Indian music and Seneta showed us how to dance. We were having a wonderful time.

Suddenly, without warning, Natalie put her hands to her ears and screamed. Miss Lavender stopped the music.

'What's the matter Nat?' asked Georgina.

'It hurts,' she said. Then something strange happened. Seneta and Melanie walked to the door and left. Just like that! Without a word!

93

'They've gone to the Centre of Excellence,' I said. 'Are you ok Nat?'

'Yes thanks,' she said. 'There was a piercing noise in my ear. It was really painful, but it's gone now.'

I looked at Miss Lavender. She pursed her lips.

'Follow them Lottie,' she urged.

*

I tiptoed down the stairs behind them, making sure they didn't see me. I followed, at a safe distance, only stopping to straighten Henry, who had egg on his face. I turned the corner but they had disappeared! I peered into the medical room. Olly the Owl was on duty.

'Yes Lottie?' she said, clasping her hands together and closing her eyes, as if she was praying.

'Er, have you got anything for a headache please?' I asked, glancing round at the cubicles for signs of anyone lurking. I could hear the familiar tap tap of Mrs Potts's fingernails, but I couldn't see anything. Miss Orrell gave me two paracetamols and a drink of water. I thanked her but, before I could pretend to take them, she snatched them back.

'Go and clean the oven out for Della. That will cure your headache. You're manners are far too nice for a bad girl.'

Drat!

As I came out of the medical room, I heard voices in the lobby. Mrs Potts was talking to some policemen so it couldn't have been her I'd heard - so much for my detective work. I wondered what they were saying so I crept nearer.

'Someone from the village you say?' said Mrs Potts, patting her purple hair. 'And what makes you think it was one of our girls?'

'The next-door neighbour says some of your girls visited at about 10.30 am, and she saw another girl later, with a dog.'

I gave a sharp intake of breath. It couldn't be …

'Well, none of our girls have pets. It's not allowed. Well thank you officer, I hope the lady recovers. Er Mrs …?'

'Foster – Winifred Foster. She's in the Infirmary and she's in a bad way.'

*

'But it *can't* be our Winnie,' wailed Georgina.

'I tell you it is,' I said, wishing I wasn't the one to tell them the bad news.

'Oh my life,' cried Topsy, still in her jim-jams.

The door burst open. Toyah walked in, chewing on some gum.

'Ever thought of knocking?' said Seneta, sarcastically.

Toyah ignored her. She turned to Topsy and Flopsy.

'Mrs Potts wants to see you two worms, after breakfast.'

'What for?' asked Flopsy. Topsy went white and clung to her sister.

'Dunno,' said Toyah, shrugging her shoulders. 'And this is for you. She handed me a letter, all the time staring as if she hated me.

'Enjoyed your party last night did you?'

I returned the stare and didn't answer - my face had turned to stone. She turned on her heels and walked out.

'What was all *that* about?' said Natalie. 'Surely Mrs Potts isn't going to blame the twins for mugging Winnie? It's absurd.'

'We haven't done anything,' moaned Topsy.

'Oh my life,' said Flopsy.

Georgina came over to me and sat on my bed.

'You *know* something don't you? More than you're telling us.'

'I heard the policeman say that some girls had visited Winnie. That was us,' I admitted.

'Yes but that doesn't prove anything. Anyway Miss Lavender will vouch for Topsy and Flopsy. They were with her all evening.'

'How can she? Nobody is supposed to know she's here. She'll lose her home if anyone finds out.'

'Are we going to prison?' whispered Topsy.

'If Winnie dies, they'll hang us,' said Flopsy, gulping. This was getting out of hand.

'STOP IT!' I shouted. 'No-one's going to prison and they abolished hanging years ago. Anyway, there's more.'

'What is it?' said Natalie, who could hear every word these days.

'The policeman said that a girl with a dog had visited as well.'

'But Cleo came with us in the morning.'

'No, not then – later.'

Seneta, who had been quiet up to now said:

'Oh that's it then. Toyah Tranter went back with your dog to steal your friend's valuables and clobbered her. That's just what I would expect from her.'

'No she didn't Seneta, I'm sure of it.' I fought back tears, not sure at all.

'You'll stick up for her - even now? You're pathetic. And how did she know about the party? You must have told her.'

I sighed. It appeared that things hadn't changed one jot.

*

I took Cleo for a walk to clear my head. I nearly forgot the letter that Toyah had given me. I was so worried about Winnie – and Toyah - and the twins. Finding it in my pocket I sat on a fallen tree and opened it while Cleo was chasing rabbits. It was from Dad and there was a twenty-pound note in it.

Hi Princess, it said, *Hope you are well and hope the money comes in useful. I can't imagine what you are spending it all on. Don't forget what we told you – be good! Things are hectic here - I'm busy decorating the lounge. Mum doesn't like the colour, it seems we can't agree on anything. She's taken Josh to stay with Gran. Got to go to work now. Love you lots! Dad xxx*

'What does it mean Cleo?' I said, anxiously. 'Why have mum and Josh gone to Gran's - surely not because of the colour of the lounge? Have they split up?'

She looked at me with her big brown sorrowful eyes. She was so trusting with her head on one side and her tongue hanging out.

'At least we can buy some more dog food!' I said as she licked away my tears. We were bringing leftovers to eke out the food we'd bought but Cleo ate like a horse and was putting on weight. It must have been all the fresh air she was getting.

We had planned to go to the hospital to see Winnie. It was Saturday and we didn't know what time visiting time was or even if they would let us in, but we had to try. However we couldn't go until we knew about the twins. They came rushing out of Mrs Potts's office in their matching blue duffle coats.

'Oh my life,' they chimed in unison and showed us a letter. It was from their old school in Essex.

'Read it, Georgie please,' Topsy begged. Georgie took the letter.'

'Hmm. *"It has come to our notice that Anastasia Winters is suffering from Dyslexia. Therefore we are willing to take her and her sister Alexandra into our school so that they can further their education as soon as possible."*

'I didn't know you were called Anastasia and Alexandra,' she said with wide eyes.

I hugged them both.

'What lovely names. Why don't you use them?'

'Mum and Dad called us after the Russian royal family,' explained Topsy.

'We felt they were too grand for this place so used our nicknames,' added her sister.

'They'll be glad to have you back, but we'll miss you,' I said. 'What do you say girls?'

'OH MY LIFE!' we all chorused.

*

The hospital was in the next town, which was about ten miles away. We didn't have to wait long at the bus stop. It was a good job because there was driving rain and a biting wind.   'I wonder if it *was* Toyah?' said Natalie, stamping her feet to keep warm.

'The evidence seems pretty conclusive,' Georgina said, pulling her 'ManU' scarf tighter round her neck.

'What does that mean?' asked Topsy.

'She means it looks like Toyah did it,' I chipped in, miserably.

The bus came and we piled on. I bought the tickets with some of Dad's money. We found the hospital and asked at the desk for Winifred Foster.

'She's very poorly, girls,' said the receptionist, kindly. 'But go down to Ward 4 and ask Sister. She may let you in.'

Sister looked at us sternly. She had her hands on her hips.

'Not likely,' she said. 'Mrs Foster needs plenty of rest. She's asleep anyway.'

'But we've come an awful long way,' I pleaded.

'And she's our friend,' said Topsy, holding up a bunch of flowers we had all helped to pay for. Sister's face softened.

'Oh all right – five minutes,' she said.

We stood looking at Winnie in silence. She had a black eye and her face was swollen. Her eyes were closed and her teeth were in a glass on the bedside table.

'It's not her!' said Flopsy.

But it was. Our lovely Winnie, all beaten and battered.

'Oh my life!'

I stroked Winnie's hair.

'Winnie,' I said gently. 'It's Lottie and Georgie. Topsy and Flopsy and Natalie are here too. Who did this to you Winnie?'

Winnie opened her eyes and looked at each of us. She knew who we were because she gave a weak smile.

'Toyah,' she started to say but fell asleep.

*

It was time for Cleo's evening walk. I crawled into the shed and jumped in surprise.

'Toyah!'

She was sitting in the corner, crying and cuddling Cleo.

'How's the old lady?'

'Like you care!'

'What? You think I did it?'

'Well didn't you? She'd shown you up earlier. You were well moody.'

'Yes I was upset. You said your best friend was the Asian, even though she doesn't speak to you. And I suppose you're best pals again now you've had that festival thing.'

I sighed.

'Toyah, I've told you, time and again, that she is Indian and her name is Seneta. How did you know about the party?'

'I guessed. I knew you were up to something. Ok, so I don't always say the right things, I'm sorry. It doesn't mean that I beat old ladies up but if that's what you want to think.'

She got up and dived through the hole, leaving me alone with Cleo.

I looked at our old tennis racquets lying on a wooden box. We hadn't played for a while, what with taking Cleo for walks and visiting Winnie. I didn't want to believe that Toyah had mugged her, but why would Winnie lie?

I thought maybe Winnie had made a mistake. After all she did get our names mixed up. Then I noticed a package, wrapped in newspaper. Tearing off the paper, I gasped. It was a little china jug with roses on the side. I recognised it immediately. The last time I'd seen it was at Winnie's house - pretty conclusive, as Georgina would say.

I couldn't sleep that night. I tossed about on my lumpy bed with things turning in my mind. First I faced Seneta; then I turned to face Georgina. The moon was shining through the thin curtains and I could just make out the shapes of two pink suitcases, all packed ready for the twins' departure. Above the gentle breathing sounds of my neighbours I could hear the clankity clanck of machinery in the distance – a noise that I couldn't explain. I buried my head in the hard pillow, determined to find out what was going on.

Chapter 10 – FIREWORKS

We missed Topsy and Flopsy after they had gone. Of course we gave them a good send off, with the help of Miss Lavender. I think she had something to do with them going - one of her letters I guess – but she wouldn't admit it. We clubbed together and bought them a pretty bracelet each and Miss Lavender gave them both a book by Jacqueline Wilson, which she signed Erica Lavender.

We stood on Platform Four ready to wave them off.

'It's time you got on the train,' said Georgie.

Topsy turned to me.

'We'll never settle until we know you and Seneta are friends again.'

'Do it for us?' pleaded Flopsy.

I tried to put the most plaintive look on my face, the one I reserve when asking Mum a special favour.

'What about it Seneta?'

'Go on, make up,' Natalie urged.

Georgina picked up the cases.

'Whatever you're doing, you'd better do it quick,' she said, lifting them onto the train.

'Will you promise not to mention the Centre of Excellence for Natural Talent?' asked Seneta.

'Ok – I promise. And will you promise not to be rude about Toyah?'

There was a long pause.

'Oh all right then but it won't stop me *thinking* rude things about her.'

'Deal.'

I held my hand out and she took it. We sort of hugged. It was a bit stiff, like grown-ups who don't really know each other but the twins were delighted and jumped onto the train.

'Give our love to Winnie!' they shouted as the train picked up speed and took them away from us. We waved until all that was left was empty tracks.

'Our butterflies have flown,' said Natalie sadly as we walked slowly away.

'Sorry about all the nasty things I said to you,' I whispered to Seneta.

'Me too,' she replied.

'And I think you'll make a great nurse.'

*

We rang the hospital every day to ask after Winnie. She gradually got better and one day they told us she was ready for home. During all this time Toyah and I had kept out of each other's way. I didn't want to think that she had mugged Winnie but, as Georgina had said, you can't argue with evidence.

On November 4th, we were getting ready to visit her at home. We had even persuaded Seneta to brave the cold wind and threatening clouds to join us. She was ready first and stood looking out of the window.

'Who are those people getting out of that black car?' she asked. 'They look official.'

We craned our necks to see. Sure enough, two men and one woman got out of the shiny car. They were all wearing dark suits and carrying briefcases. Creeping downstairs we hid, out of sight near the lobby.

'We would like to see Mrs Potts please,' said the lady.

'Who shall I say wants her?' asked Ollie the Owl, who had opened the door.

'Tell her it's the school inspectors.'

'School inspectors – no way!' said Natalie, who could now hear the slightest whisper.

'We must tell Hammy,' I said, urgently. Hammy was our pet name for Miss Lavender. I wondered if this could be her doing.

'You must do everything you can to alert them to the wrongdoings at this school,' she said when we told her. She had a stern look on her face.

We put off our visit to Winnie until after school time and attended all the lessons we were supposed to attend. We were determined to show the inspectors how stupid the rules were but the teachers must have had an emergency plan. They started acting like it was a normal school! They even opened a room we hadn't been inside before. It was full of brand new computers! I managed a quick email to Josh while I was in there. I knew he would be tickled pink.

We were given lines for being cheeky, detention for being late and Melanie got sent to Mrs Potts for smoking in the classroom!

'It's not working,' I whispered during Art. The inspectors were in the room and we were getting nowhere. Seneta got one hundred house points for a drawing she did of me. She made me look quite attractive and I was delighted. Natalie was praised for being helpful and handing out materials. It was hopeless. My hand shot up.

'Yes, Charlotte?' said Mr Brock.

'Why don't we practice signatures Sir?' I asked, sweetly.

'Don't be silly Charlotte,' he said, clearing his throat. He turned to the inspectors.

'They do come out with the silliest things.' The men in dark suits smiled and the woman with the clipboard, and just a hint of moustache, nodded as if she knew all about children.

At lunchtime, we were surprised to see the three witches looking clean and presentable. We had tomato soup, which was actually red, followed by fish that tasted like fish, mashed potatoes (with almost no lumps) and peas, which were quite easily speared with a fork. For sweet there was fresh fruit. It was the best meal we had eaten since we started the school. I saw the inspectors tucking in and chatting as if they were satisfied that all was well.

'We've got to do something,' I said, feeling exasperated.

'Like what?' asked Seneta.

Georgie's eyes widened.

'The moonshine!'

I gave her a high five.

Natalie and Seneta looked puzzled. We told them about the whisky in the stables.

'So, are we going to tell the inspectors about it?' asked Natalie, puzzled.

'Better than that,' said Georgie, with mischief written all over her bespectacled face. 'We all tell one other person and tell them *not* to tell anyone.'

Seneta screwed up her nose.

'How will that alert the inspectors?'

'You'll see,' I grinned at Georgie. 'Let's split. Don't tell any prefects though!'

It was just my luck to bump into Penelope Freestone. I looked round, safety in numbers and all that but there was no one in sight!

She made a beeline for me.

'What's this? Grottie Lottie on her own – without her mates to protect her. The girl who befriends everyone – prefects – dogs – old ladies with cats!

So it was Penelope who had been lurking near Winnie's house!

'You don't scare me!'

She thumped and kicked in her usual unladylike manner. I could have sent her scurrying but I pretended to be scared.

'Leave me alone, please! I'll tell you a secret.'

She stopped at once.

'There's a still in the old stables,' I said. 'And loads of bottles of whisky.'

'Pull the other one,' she said, grabbing hold of my spiky hair.

'It's true – honest!'

'You had better be right, or I'll kill you next time,' she snarled.

'But you won't tell anyone will you?'

107

'What do you think?' she replied, and ran back to her friends.

'What happened to you?' asked Seneta when we all met up again.

'Penelope Freestone, that's what! How did you get on?'

'Me and Nat went in Klepto toilets and saw that two doors were closed. We talked about the whisky and pretended to be surprised when the girls came out. We made them promise not to tell anyone.

'Cool,' said Georgina. 'I saw Melanie and told her. Before she was out of sight, I saw her whispering to another girl from Arson. Then I saw Suzanne Charlton from Truant and I told her. She said she wouldn't tell a living soul!'

'I still don't understand,' wailed Natalie.

'Watch and learn girl,' said Georgie, mimicking Brock the Badger. 'Watch and learn!'

By the time the bell rang for afternoon lessons, the whole school knew about the whisky. Many of them had visited the stables and had obviously tried the moonshine for themselves. Some girls were tottering when they came into Maths. Others fell asleep in the middle of Pythagoras's Theorem. We were delighted! Olly the Owl said there must be a bug going round and the inspectors were scribbling notes for all they were worth

After detention, we reported to Miss Lavender. She was very pleased with us.

'Well done!' she said. 'Everyone with a secret tells just one person and swears them to secrecy. That's how rumours spread. Let's hope the inspectors were unimpressed and make some changes around here. I don't suppose you've been to the Centre of Excellence today Seneta?'

'No,' she said, frowning. 'I was talking to Melanie about it. You would have thought Mrs Potts would have wanted to show off her star pupils, wouldn't you?'

'Hmm,' said Mrs Lavender, looking at me knowingly.

I laughed.

'I expect Mr and Mrs Potty features have had their hands full, getting rid of the whisky still. Most of the school is drunk and I heard that Potts was last seen pouring bottles of you-know-what into the brook.'

We laughed until we cried.

'And Fishy Haddock nearly wet her knickers when she found out the girls had found her secret supply. I reckon she found the whisky ages ago and has been helping herself ever since,' said Georgina, with tears streaming down her face.

We were all helpless. My stomach ached with laughing.

'As a point of interest,' said Miss Lavender, dabbing the corner of her eyes with a tissue. 'Have you got a nickname for me? You seem to have one for everyone else.'

'Of course not,' said Georgina, but her cheeks went pink.

'Oh, that's rather disappointing' Miss Lavender pouted her lips.

'We sometimes call you Hammy Hamster,' I ventured, holding my breath for her reaction. 'Because you come out at night.'

She pretended to look sternly from one to the other of us but couldn't keep a straight face.

'I suppose I must be grateful that it's a cute furry animal,' she said, laughing. 'I could have been the old bat!'

*

We didn't bother with tea but decided to get some chips in the village instead. I was looking forward to seeing Winnie and even persuaded Seneta to come along. We called to feed Cleo first and take her with us. I thought she would be ready for a walk because we didn't dare with the inspectors around. When we got to the shed, Cleo wasn't there.

'Toyah must have taken her,' I said, wondering where she had gone.

Because the farm would be extra muddy after a lot of rain, we walked the long way round, arriving at Winnie's front door just as her neighbour was coming out.

'More visitors, Winnie,' the rather large woman called. She told us to go on in.

As soon as we opened the door, Cleo came bounding up to me, jumping up and barking.

'Cleo, what are you doing here?' I asked as I petted her. It was then that I saw Toyah. She was picking up an ornament of a Siamese cat.

'What are *you* doing here and what are you doing with *that*?' I asked, remembering the little jug in the shed.

'I'm only dusting it,' was the curt reply. 'And I've got as much right here as you!'

Toyah – dusting? No way.

'Come on in,' said Winnie. 'And leave Toyah alone. She's been here all day and has been a real help. She's even done some baking.'

We went to see Winnie in the other room and gave her a gentle hug. She seemed so fragile; I was frightened of breaking her.

'Oh it's good to see you Winnie,' I said. 'I hope you're feeling better. This is Seneta, by the way.'

'So this is the famous Seneta,' said Winnie taking her hand. Seneta smiled.

'What's Toyah doing here?' whispered Georgina. 'When we came to the hospital and Lottie asked you who'd done that terrible thing to you, you said Toyah.'

'Did I? I must have been confused. I was very tired. I was trying to remember all your names and Toyah was the missing one.'

Toyah had followed us into the room.

'But I heard the policeman say that someone had come back here later, with a dog,' I accused.

Toyah sat on the arm of Winnie's chair.

'I did come back with Cleo. I came to say I was sorry for being so rude. I wasn't born with bad manners you know. My Nan taught me to respect old people.

'And the jug?' I asked. I had to be sure she was telling the truth.

'I gave her the jug,' said Winnie. 'Toyah told me all about her grandma dying and said that she

111

had a jug just like mine. I told her she could have it and she could come round any time. She is going to stay with me at Christmas. We're going to have a lovely time, just you and me, aren't we love?' She raised her hand and Toyah took hold of it.

'Yes Winnie,' she said, looking at Winnie fondly.

I couldn't believe it. 'Sorry for not believing you,' I said and really meant it. 'I'm glad it wasn't you.'

'I'm sorry too,' said Georgina. We got you wrong.'

'Me too,' said Natalie.

I looked at Seneta.

'And me most of all,' she said. 'Sorry Toyah.'

'It's my own fault,' Toyah said, matter-of-factly. 'For stealing your purses on your first day. I took it out on all of you because I felt sorry for myself.'

'Well that's that,' said Winnie, smiling. 'Now, let's have a nice cup of tea and one of Toyah's rock cakes. Where are the twins by the way?'

'They've gone home, lucky things,' I said. 'But they sent their love.'

Toyah handed round the cakes and we all took a bite – or should I say, *tried* to take a bite. I nearly broke my teeth.

'I'd stick to dusting if I was you.'

Toyah stuck out her tongue.

'Now that's the Toyah we know and love,' said the ever-wise Georgina, dumping her cake in the bin.

*

As we were trudging back up the drive to the school, a police car passed us, going the other way.

'Blimey, the Freestone Three were in that car!' said Georgie. We cheered.

'Good,' said Toyah. 'I think they followed us when we went to Winnie's house that day. And I saw them later when I cut through the farm. Also Winnie said her attackers were three girls with lots of metal in their faces.'

'That certainly fits the Freestone Three,' I said. 'Come to think of it, Penny mentioned Winnie this morning, when we had our little chat.'

'But who told the police?' asked Seneta.

'Me,' replied Toyah, proudly.

*

There was more excitement the following day. Mr and Mrs Potts came into breakfast. The food was back to its normal standard – burnt toast, watery scrambled egg and lumpy porridge. They announced that they were going away for a while, leaving Miss Orrell in charge.

'I don't suppose we will ever find out about the Centre of Excellence now,' complained Miss Lavender, when Georgie and I went up to give her the news.

'I'm not so sure,' I replied. 'When Seneta wanted to show off to the inspectors yesterday, it was Olly the Owl who told her to shut up.

113

'Mmm, interesting,' she said. 'Lottie, what are you doing?'

'Sorry,' I replied, thoughtfully. I was levelling a picture that wasn't straight. She must have moved it when she was dusting. It reminded me of the picture of Henry the Eight at the bottom of the stairs. I was always straightening that too. I ran down the stairs two at a time to take another look.

As usual, Henry stood with his hands on his hips smiling down at me. I levelled the frame once again. There was something about this corner of the stairwell that puzzled me. This was where the girls disappeared after the Divali party. I pressed the wood panelling around him, looking for a secret passage. Nothing happened.

'You know what this is about, don't you Henry? You see everything that goes on. Can't you give me a clue? You are always grinning at me as if you have a secret. And you are a messy boy!'

Wiping porridge off his bearded chin with a tissue, the picture wobbled. I lifted the frame, realising that there was something underneath. Just under the left hand corner was a button.

'So, you *are* hiding a secret!' I accused. 'Shame on you!'

I felt my heart flutter as I pressed the button. A panel slid open in the corridor and I slipped inside, pressing another button to close it. I was in a sort of workroom. There were tables, littered with all sorts of pens and inks. A thin cord was stretched across the room and bits of paper were pegged on to it, like washing. In the fireplace there was a large machine. It looked like a printing machine. I gasped.

'They're making money!' I whispered to myself in disbelief.

I heard a tap-tap-tap coming from next door like last time in the Medical Room. I couldn't understand it at first. Mrs Potts did that with her nails but she had left that morning. Wondering if she had secretly returned, I hid behind a filing cabinet.

'I tell you it's too dangerous,' said a voice that I recognised. It was Ann Asquith, Miss Dairy Box herself!

'Seneta is beginning to ask a lot of questions. I think her silicone chip is weakening.'

'I know. She only wanted to show the inspectors what we were doing! That was very awkward, I can tell you. It's that friend of hers, Lottie. She's too nosy for her own good. I'm sure she suspects something. *She* tried to make me look silly in front of the inspectors. I've tried to improve her skills so that we could recruit her but she's hopeless. Not an artistic bone in her body.'

Brock the Badger! I couldn't believe it. That's why he was making me do signatures on my Birthday. Of course, then I remembered that he tapped on the desk with his pencil just like Mrs Potts did with her nails! It must have been him I could hear from the Medical Room.

'Mavis said it was too dangerous to continue,' Miss Asquith said, 'What with the inspectors coming and the police questioning everyone about that mugging. She said we had better wait until it's all died down.'

I couldn't think who Mavis was.

'But we're so close,' said Mr Brock. 'Just one more session and we'll have enough money to retire to the Bahamas. We can give Seneta another implant to shut her up. Then we can get out of this lousy place. We can split the money up two ways instead of three. We deserve it if we're prepared to take more risks. We'll be miles away before Mavis Orrell finds out.'

'Oh, I don't know,' Miss Asquith whined. 'The implants are only in the experimental stage. What if Seneta is brain damaged?'

I had to clap my hand over my mouth when I heard that, I can tell you.

'All the girls in this school are brain damaged, if you ask me. Come on Annie – then we can be together. Pick up the microphone and give one last order.'

There was silence for a few minutes as if she was deciding what to do. Then a loud crackly sound filled the room. It was Miss Asquith's voice.

'*My gels*,' she said. *'It is time once again for your special task. Come at once to the CENT Room. Don't tell anyone where you are going. Don't let anyone see you. They are the enemy. You are better than them. They are nothing.'*

So that's how they did it. The girls must have received messages through the implant in their head. Natalie's hearing aid must have picked up the signal at the Divali party. I squeezed back out of the wooden panel, just in time to hide behind a pillar and watch girls coming from all directions. The leader, Erin Jones, pressed the button under Henry the Eighth and left him wonky again. They all looked like robots. Seneta and Melanie were at the back. I ran up to them and tried to pull them away but it was no good; it was as if they hadn't seen me. I needed to phone the police but I couldn't do it from school. It was too dangerous.

When they had disappeared behind the secret panel, I ran upstairs and rummaged in Seneta's drawer for her mobile. It wasn't there. She had taken it with her!

I ran downstairs and saw a girl I knew from Truant. I knew she had a mobile. She was talking to some Klepto girls. When I stopped her, they scarpered.

'Could I borrow your phone please, Zoe?' I asked. 'It's very important.'

'It's got no money on it, Lottie' she said.

'999 doesn't cost anything,' I told her. '*Please* let me borrow it!'

'Crikey! What are you ringing 999 for?'

'Zoe – please!'

'Ok.'

She felt in the left pocket of her denim jacket. It wasn't there. She felt in her right pocket. It wasn't there either.

'Oh no, those girls from Klepto have stolen it!'

I ran after them shouting 'STOP THIEVES!' They ran off but I soon caught them up. My karate lessons came in very handy. It's amazing how a

117

few noises and a confident raise of a flat hand can scare the pants of the toughest of them. They soon threw down the phone and ran away. I dialled 999. Nothing! The battery had gone! I gave it back to Zoe and ran down the drive to the phone box on the lane. I passed some girls from Grievous on the way and asked them if they had a mobile.

'Get lost!' was my answer. I should have known.

A whoosh in the sky made me jump out of my skin. Of course - it was bonfire night! I thought of Cleo and hoped she would be all right. Reaching the telephone booth, I wasn't surprised to find that it had been vandalised. There was nothing for it but to run all the way to the village.

It was freezing cold and I hadn't got a coat on. Rockets were whizzing all about me and I had the stitch. I took the shortcut through the farm and a huge dog frightened the life out of me but I kept running. My feet squelched and slurped in the mud making it difficult to pick my legs up. It seemed to take forever to get there but I eventually spotted the old red phone box on the village green, praying that it would work.

I dialled 999 and a lady's voice answered:

'Which service do you require?'

'Police please, and hurry!'

I was out of breath and couldn't stop shaking. A deep voice came on the line and I told him about the counterfeit money and the implants. It must have sounded very farfetched.

'I'm sorry,' he said. 'We have orders to take emergency calls from Mr and Mrs Potts only. We have had too many hoax calls from that school of late.'

'But they left this morning, and my friend is in danger of being brain damaged,' I screamed, hysterically.

'All right, all right, calm down - I'll send someone to investigate. But you'll be in big trouble, young lady, if this is a hoax. First tell me your name.'

I thanked him and set off back to the school. I could see a glow in the sky. Bonfire Night was in full swing now. I needed to check on Cleo. I could hear sirens in the distance and felt reassured that the Police had responded to my call. I reached the shed and gave Cleo her tea.

'I'll come back in a little while,' I said, wishing I had a radio to hide the noise. 'We'll go for a walk later when the rockets have quietened down.'

She whined as I pulled the wood back in place to stop her getting out and I felt really guilty. There was nothing for it but to take her with me. We ran through the woods and, once in the open, I couldn't believe my eyes. The school was on fire! Girls and firemen were all over the place. Miss Orrell was ticking everyone off on a clipboard. I tied Cleo to a tree and ran up to her.

'Ah – Charlotte Longfellow – I wondered where you were. I've nearly got everyone now. There's just Seneta Sharma, Melanie Pearson ...'

'There's the whole Centre for Natural Bloomin' Talent!' I screamed at her.

119

She grabbed hold of my arm and pulled me to one side.

'What do you mean?'

'They're in there now, with Dairy, I mean Miss Asquith and Mr Brock. They mean to double cross you. And they're going to give Seneta another implant – she'll end up brain dead unless you do something about it! That is if she doesn't burn alive first. They're trapped in there. They won't know the building is on fire!'

She pushed me out of the way.

'Double cross me eh? We'll see about that!'

She walked over to a big burley fireman and told him how to get into the room. After what seemed like hours, but was probably only a few minutes, they came out, coughing and spluttering from the thick black smoke. Miss Asquith and Mr Brock emerged to find a very angry Miss Orrell waiting for them. Seneta was taken to an ambulance with Melanie and the other Centre of Excellence girls. I went and put my arm round her.

'Are you all right?' I asked. She nodded.

'Oh Lottie, is Hammy safe?' she asked in a croaky voice.

I had forgotten all about Miss Lavender! I ran towards the front door. A fireman pulled me back.

'You can't go in there love,' he said.

'But there's a teacher up there!'

Ollie the Owl joined us.

'No Charlotte,' she said. 'Everyone is accounted for.'

At that moment Miss Lavender appeared at the attic window, high in the West Tower. She opened it and waved. Someone shouted 'It's the White Lady!'

I screamed. It was much too high for her to jump and flames were licking round her from the floor below. She smiled down at me and I had a strange feeling that I couldn't explain. She blew me a kiss and turned away. The firemen acted quickly. They backed a big fire engine up to the building and extended the long ladder. A brave fireman climbed slowly up to her room and disappeared into the swirling black smoke. He came down alone.

'There's no-one there,' he said as he tore off his helmet and stared at the building. I looked up at the window for a long time before a kind fireman put a blanket round my shoulders and told me he was taking me to safety.

BAD SCHOOL

CHAPTER 11 – REUNITED

We sat huddled together in the makeshift dormitory, which had been set up in the church hall.

'Do you think she's dead?' asked Natalie, her face as white as the day we first met Miss Lavender.

'The fireman would have found her if she was,' said Georgina, practical as ever.

'So where did she go?' Natalie persisted.

'I don't think she existed,' I said. They looked at me as if I'd gone bonkus.

'You mean she really *was* a ghost?' Natalie's voice rose hysterically. Her pale face looked more ghostly than ever Miss Lavender did.

'Shh,' said Georgina. 'She may have found another way out. She wasn't supposed to be there remember?'

Natalie and I looked at one another. Neither of us believed that anyone could have got out of there alive.

All the ladies of the village brought sandwiches and soup. Mr Singh from the shop brought sweets and crisps. They all felt sorry for us but once we had got over our fright we began to relax and enjoy ourselves. It was like a big sleepover.

'Fancy old Dairy Box and Mr Brock!' said Georgina, tucking into a cheese and tomato sarnie.

'Do you think they kiss and - stuff?' asked Natalie, screwing up her nose.

'Suppose so,' I said. 'What a horrible thought! I suppose he gave her all those chocolates.'

Someone wheeled in a telly and we watched an old episode of 'Only Fools and Horses. At 10 o'clock, the news came on. The main story was about us!

'A girls' school in Dorset has caught fire,' the reporter said. *'Several girls are being treated in hospital, suffering from minor burns, smoke inhalation and shock. They are being kept in for observation. It is thought that the fire was caused by fireworks being set off inside the building.'*

'I bet it started in Arson,' someone said, 'Pyromaniacs the lot of them.'

'I heard it started in Truant,' said someone else, probably from Arson.

The reporter continued:

'We have just received a statement from the police in the picturesque village of Grimstone, near to the school of the same name. It says that three teachers have been arrested for printing counterfeit banknotes. Apparently, while the fire was raging, one of the girls was desperately trying to convince the police that a society called the Centre of Excellence for Natural Talent was the front for this crime. They used talented girls by implanting a microchip into their neck and hypnotising them. The girls will need a minor operation to remove the implants. A spokesman for the hospital stated that, had anything gone wrong with these implants, it could have resulted in brain damage.'

The place was in uproar – the noise was deafening.

'You suspected all along, didn't you, Lottie?' said Georgina, patting me on the back. 'Poor Seneta.'

'You should get a medal,' Natalie suggested.

I didn't answer. I was thinking about Miss Lavender and Seneta – and Melanie and the others of course.

All the commotion upset Cleo who was cuddled up in my sleeping bag. The friendly fireman had helped me to smuggle her into the hall under his big coat. She started barking under my blanket and I had to pretend to cough violently in an attempt to cover up the noise. Miss Goldsmith, thinking I must have caught a chill, made me drink some horrible medicine. Yuk. She appeared to be as surprised as everyone else by the TV report though, and was quite friendly towards us.

*

By morning, worried parents had begun to arrive to pick up their daughters. Georgina's dad was one of the first. After a tearful greeting she asked:

'Where's your girlfriend then?'

'Oh, she's gone,' he said, grinning. 'She gave me the needle!'

Georgina was delighted. We suddenly realised that we mightn't see one another again and hurriedly swapped addresses. Nat's parents came next. They were upset and tearful, blaming themselves for not noticing that Nat was deaf. Apparently, someone had written to them only two days before to inform them that she was a bright girl who had been held back because of her hearing. Good old Miss Lavender.

*

More and more girls left and I wondered what would happen to me. I took Cleo for a walk and called in to see Winnie. Toyah was still there. She had stayed the night and was helping Winnie look for her teeth!

'Take care, Winnie,' I said, with tears in my eyes and a lump in my throat. 'And thanks for everything.'

'You too, Lottie,' she said, gumily. 'Whatever you do with your life; do it well.'

I flung my arms around her neck and kissed her.

'I don't know what that will be, Winnie. I'm no good at anything.'

'Nonsense girl,' she spluttered. 'Don't put yourself down. You're good with people. You *care*. That's a very special talent. You could be an air hostess or a social worker, in fact anything you want.'

'Do you really think so?'

'Of course - I don't thsay things I don't mean! Oh, you'll have to take me to the dentist Toyah, to get some new teeth.'

She was looking under cushions and in the cat basket. I turned to Toyah

'What will you do now?' I asked.

'She's going to stay with me until she can bake as well as me,' said Winnie, offering me a

126

biscuit after making sure her teeth weren't in the tin.

'Thanks. That will be a long time then.' I winked at her.

'Suits me,' said Toyah, grinning like a Cheshire cat. 'Winnie's like the family I always wanted. I'll write to mum and tell her where I'm staying but she won't bother.'

She came with me to the door.

'So why didn't you tell me about this woman who's been teaching you?'

'Miss Lavender? I wanted to, Toyah, but I'd promised I wouldn't tell anyone. You understand that don't you?'

'Suppose so. It wasn't Miss Lavender anyway. I could have told you that. She died two years' ago in a road accident.'

I decided not to argue and shrugged my shoulders.

'It must have been someone else then. Anyway what have you done with Winnie's teeth?' I whispered.

'Oh, I buried them in the garden,' was her surprising reply. 'If I'm staying here, I can't put up with all that clicking and clacking. They fell out in her hot chocolate last night!'

'But what if she finds out?' I asked. I was worried that the new friendship might end in tears.

'She knows I've hidden them to get her to the dentist,' said Toyah. 'Just like I know that the cooking lessons are her way of giving me a home.'

127

'It sounds like you two are made for each other. By the way Toyah - is it all right to take Cleo home with me?'

'Only if you bring her for a visit sometime,'

'It's a deal,' I said.

*

As I reached the church hall, I saw Dad's car. Before I knew it I was wrapped in the arms of Mum, Dad and Josh. Josh wiped an arm across his eyes.

'What's up with you little bro?' I asked, through a curtain of mist.

'Something in my eye,' he mumbled. Then he saw Cleo.

'Whose is it?' he asked, stooping down to fuss her.

'Mine,' I answered, avoiding Dad's eyes.

'OH NO IT ISN'T!'

'Please Dad,' I begged. I couldn't bear to part with her. 'If you don't let me keep her, I'll go and live at Gran's with Mum and Josh.' I knew Gran wouldn't mind.

'What *are* you talking about?' Mum was puzzled.

They all looked at me as if I'd dyed my hair pink or something (not a bad idea, actually). But all the worries about my parents splitting up came bubbling up to the surface. I started to cry.

'What's up Princess?' asked Dad, stroking my hair.

'In your last letter, you said Mum and Josh had gone to live with Gran.' I accused.

'Only while I decorated the house - the paint was aggravating Josh's asthma!

'You'll have to let her keep the dog now,' said Josh playfully punching Dad on the arm, 'for causing all that worry.'

I couldn't believe it. My dirty, smelly, foul-mouthed brother was actually sticking up for me. He must have missed me as much as I missed him! I looked at Dad and knew he couldn't hold out for long against the two of us.

'Please Dad.'

He looked at Mum. His eyebrows were raised in an unspoken question. She smiled and nodded.

'Oh all right then!' Dad said. 'But you'll have to look after it and take it for walks – it looks a bit overweight!'

We had a big family hug, with Cleo barking in the middle of us. I was so happy, I thought it was the wrong time to point out to Dad that Cleo was a girl and not an 'it'.

*

Seneta came back home after having the implant removed and she is her old self again. Our parents took us back to the old school last week to see Miss Armitage. We sat in the brightly polished office and studied our shoes once again. But instead of giving us a lecture, Miss Armitage was actually quite nice.

'We made a terrible mistake by sending you to Grimstone Priory,' she said, peering over her half moon glasses. 'We would be happy for you to return to this school.'

'But we don't want old feuds to start up again,' said Mr. Sharma with creases on his brow. My Dad agreed.

'It might be better if they made a fresh start in a new school.'

'With no old scores to settle,' added Mum.

Seneta's parents nodded agreement. Miss Armitage sat with her elbows on the desk; her fingers joined at the tips.

'I quite understand your reasons for feeling this way. And of course you must do what you think best for your children. But it may help your decision if I tell you that Tara Walker and Katy Underwood were excluded last week. It has come to our notice that they have been bullying for some time.'

It was all we could do to stop ourselves from kissing her. We start back in the New Year when she has all the paperwork sorted. Until then we're on holiday – hurrah.

Josh has behaved perfectly since I came back. It's unreal. I have an uneasy feeling every time I open a drawer or go into my room but he just smiles sweetly and says he's glad to have me back. I truly think he's growing up.

I must tell you about Cleo. Dad loves her to bits. He took her to a vet for a check up and a diet but she wasn't getting fat from eating too many biscuits – she was pregnant! Toyah was delighted when I rang to tell her. Winnie said she could have one of the puppies. They are coming to stay with us at Christmas and Seneta is cool with this.

Mr and Mrs Sharma were dead impressed when she told them about the Divali party. They are joining us for Christmas dinner so it will be brill! Mum says she's no idea where everyone is going to sit but I don't care. We're going to have roast turkey, chestnut stuffing, roast potatoes and sprouts with lashings of gravy - scrumptious!

Mum and Dad are ok now. Apparently they were arguing because they were worried about me. How about that! They are very proud of me for what I did at the school – cool eh?

Miss Lavender was never found but she keeps a special place in our hearts. All the girls from the dorm have promised to keep in touch and I know that whenever one of us has a problem, somebody is bound to say 'What would Miss Lavender advise us to do?' I also know that whatever I do in the future, I will never forget her. And if she really was a ghost, well that's ok with me!

We are going to see my Gran in Birmingham later on this morning. Mum says I can ring Georgie and arrange to meet her while we're there. That's when I'm dressed and I have found my… ugh, what is that? I don't believe it!

'JOSH WHERE ARE YOU? WAIT TILL I GET YOU!'

Ooh, I wish Natalie were here, she would know what to do – she actually *likes* frogs.

'JOSH, COME HERE THIS MINUTE AND REMOVE THIS CREATURE FROM MY BED!'

Ah well, it's good to be home.'